# A Modern Myth: Nada's Secret

Jude Liebermann

Published by Lee Books
Austin, TX
www.readatleebooks.com


All Rights Reserved
Printed in the United States of America
Cover models originally created by Farconville on
FreeDigitalPhotos.net

ISBN (paperback) 978-0-9660653-3-6

# Prologue

Over an hour before Dawn with the park deserted, even the animals were quiet. No joggers could be seen making use of any of the trails. The clear night sky exposed the full moon shining brightly. Its beams illuminated a small woman lying behind a bench. Her pale skin and dark mahogany brown hair glistened, as her breathing grew uneasy. If anyone had happened by, they would have noticed two things about the woman: her presence in the park at such an hour and her nakedness.

She moaned and shifted as she placed a hand to her head and pushed up to a sitting position. Taking a deep breath, she opened her eyes and looked around. Obviously disoriented, she tried to recognize her surroundings. Finally looking up and gazing upon the moon, she groaned.

"Oh, hell!" She stood quickly and broke into a sprint. She ran faster than most animals, and it only took a few minutes to reach her apartment building. She bit her lip and looked around before jumping up to catch the fire escape ladder. She quickly climbed the two flights to her apartment, where her open window awaited her. Once inside, she closed the window and locked it.

## Chapter One

Nada Berch grasped the end of the warm sheet and fanned the air in front of her. The sheet spread out across the bed before slowly lowering to its surface. Nada smoothed it down and then tucked the hem beneath the mattress. She glanced at the clock beside the bed. Its digital readout displayed the time of 1:16 PM.

Nada knew she needed to get ready soon for her shift at the hospital, where she worked as an ER nurse. She sighed and looked back at the bed. She had always loved the smell of clean sheets. She stretched out on her stomach and buried her face, inhaling deeply. Nada sighed as she rolled over and stared up at the ceiling. Normally, the poster tacked there made her smile, but this time she just stared at it. She had hoped that doing the laundry would keep her mind off the night before, but it hadn't worked.

"Good morning, Sunshine." She said with a small amount of sarcasm, knowing morning had passed and that the day wouldn't be such a good one. The vampire in the poster wore the same outfit as on the television show named after him. Dressed like her dark mood, he wore a black trench coat over black pants and shirt. She preferred to wear that color as well, though she had more in common with him than that.

Nada groaned and looked away from the ceiling, as she tried to remember the night before. *Damn the full moon*, she thought. One day she would get caught running around the city naked and never work another day in her life. Nada did not want to spend the rest of her life locked in a cage or worse. *Or worse* scared her the most.

She sat up with a groan and stared down at her pale shapely legs. Her small stature at just over five feet was very deceptive, since her strength rivaled most men. Nada looked at her hands and stretched them out in front of her. She looked from her well-groomed nails around to her palms. She had noticed her missing ring when she woke and wondered where it would eventually be found. Her necklace was missing as well, and Nada's hand rose to her neck and absently traced her collarbones with her thumb and middle finger. She already checked her living room for the jewelry before remembering she had worked the night before. Nada took a deep breath and sighed.

Deciding she had wasted enough time, she headed for the kitchen. She pulled open the refrigerator and reached for a container. Her hand stopped less than an inch in front of it, and Nada realized she didn't need it.

She closed the fridge and leaned against it. She hadn't seen her kill in the park that morning, but there must have been one. She knew of no other reason why she wouldn't want the contents of the container. Ordinarily, she always started her day by drinking a cupful of the red liquid. Nada closed her eyes and again tried to remember the night before. What animal had been her victim? She knew it couldn't be human, since her own morals wouldn't allow that. After all, she herself was human. At least, she still hoped so and ignored the voice that said she hadn't been human the night before.

Still feeling disoriented, she decided to go for a run. She had plenty of time before work, since her shift didn't start for over an hour. Nada smiled as she headed outside. A hard run and then a nice long shower were just what she needed.

Nada had almost ten minutes to spare when she checked into her ward at the hospital. After stowing her personal things in her locker, she headed to the restroom. She always found it hard to deal with the first day after a full moon. Normally, they didn't take her by surprise, but she'd been distracted the previous night. At least she could remember being at work. There had been a terrible multiple car crash, and they asked her to stay late to help.

As she stared into the mirror above the sink, Nada's breathing became irregular. She suddenly remembered she hadn't felt well and went to the restroom to splash water on her face. At first she thought the sight of so much blood troubled her, but she looked at her hands cupping the water and understood. Her fingers blurred in front of her eyes as she *changed*. After looking out the window and seeing the full moon, her last human thought had been, *oh how could I forget?*

Nada angrily wiped a hand across her face, suddenly feeling stupid. Maybe she belonged in one of those cages that she feared, and she forced herself to calm down. She now knew where she lost her necklace and ring.

She looked around the floor of the restroom and then checked each stall. Nada finally found her ring in the last one, even though she couldn't remember going into the stall. The last stall also had a window, so she must have moved closer to it. She slid the ring onto her right hand and continued to look for her necklace. Her gaze fell on the trashcan, and she cringed. Her uniform had to be somewhere as well. Had she still been in the state of mind to hide it? She hesitantly walked over to the can, praying that the janitor hadn't come in yet. After she took a deep breath, she opened the lid. When she saw all the trash, she sighed in relief. The restroom must have been cleaned just before she had been there the night before. Nada pushed aside paper towels and tissues then sighed as she saw her nametag staring back at her from the bottom of the can. She grabbed her white nurse's uniform and pulled. Her broken necklace came with it and landed on the floor. Groaning, she knelt down to pick up the ruined chain and threw it back into the trash. She should stop buying necklaces, since they were too fragile.

Nada made a quick stop at her locker before heading to the main desk. She shoved the crumpled uniform in and slammed the door, leaning against the locker to take a deep breath. She tried not to think about what would have happened had another woman walked into the restroom during her *change*. Nada looked away from the ceiling and stared down the hallway. Due to her panic, she would now be late for her shift. Used to Nada relieving her early, Mia would be impatient.

"Hell, girl, what took you so long?" Mia asked as soon as she saw Nada approaching. "I got a hot date that I need to get ready for."

Nada smiled at her co-worker and looked at her watch. "How hot can it be to start so early?"

"Girl, please, I need several hours to get ready! You know I gotta look *cute!*" She finished with an exaggerated emphasis on cute, and Nada's smile got broader as she watched her. Mia, an attractive dark-skinned woman in her mid-twenties, always had an entertaining story to tell. Nada enjoyed her sense of humor and liked to relieve her early; however, her current mood didn't feel up for a story. She hoped the day wouldn't be busy and took a deep breath. If her normal luck held, there would be at least two emergencies. She would just have to concentrate and stop thinking about the previous night.

"Well, you still have plenty of time." Nada replied with an apologetic smile. " I had to make a pit stop."

"What are you, a race car driver?" Mia asked as she signed her last few reports. She chuckled to herself, as she handed the duty roster over to Nada. "Well, it's all yours, girlfriend. Have fun." She turned to leave but paused. "You *are* going with us on Friday, right?"

Nada nodded as she looked over the log. "Yeah, I'll be there."

"You better! Don't make me come get you." Mia winked and walked off. Nada looked up and watched her with envy. Mia had the luxury of being a normal woman who didn't have to worry about *changing*. Nada could no longer say that. She looked at her hand that held the pen and again wondered what had happened during the full moon.

As her hand shook, she couldn't control the shiver that ran down her spine. She dropped the pen and looked in the direction Mia had gone. It would get busy in a few hours, but Nada currently had the ward to herself. When the roads got packed due to rush hour, so would the corridors. She knew that if she walked down that corridor and took a left, she would see many people.

Busy no matter the hour, she had helped out in the emergency room the night before. Since she made sure she wouldn't be working during the full moon, she should have known better. She had been leaving when she heard the commotion from the ER and took that left, instead of going right to the parking lot. Total mayhem had erupted, and they asked her to stay. She had been able to do just that for almost two hours. Nada sighed as she remembered telling the nurse on duty that she had to leave, since she felt ill. The nurse smiled and thanked her for all her help. Relieved that she hadn't just freaked out and run from the room, Nada wouldn't have to explain any strange behavior. She had calmly left the ER and headed for the restroom in her ward.

Try as she might, Nada could not remember what happened after she splashed water on her face and began to *change*. She only had patches of memory after that. From previous experiences, she knew she would never remember what she did during a full moon. The first few times had terrified her. She thought she lost time and couldn't understand why she woke up naked in a strange place. Sometimes, she even awoke in her own living room, but it took several months before she figured it out. By then, she discovered she could *change* any time she wanted to. Only during the full moon she couldn't control it.

Nada wondered what animal she had killed the night before. Was it new or one that she had already fed upon? She knew that given enough time, she would realize what animal had been her victim. After all, the poor thing became a part of her.

# Chapter Two

The day went by as normally as any other. The hours flew by, and Nada began to feel like her old self again. Her disorientation began to fade as she struggled to put the full moon behind her. At a quarter of eleven Nada looked up to see Dr. Thorton approaching. He'd been in the ER the night before. He was in his mid-thirties and had a ruggedly handsome face and unfashionably long light-brown hair, and Nada had witnessed plenty of nurses trying to catch the handsome doctor's attention. Since they were such opposites, she could never understand why he kept trying to date her. Maybe he thought his dark complexion would complement her pale one, or maybe he just liked the challenge of dating the new girl. Either way, Nada liked the attention, even though she wasn't interested in anything other than a professional relationship. She smiled as he drew nearer.

"Hello, Nada. I wanted to thank you for helping out last night. Your help was invaluable."

"You're welcome, Dr. Thorton. I'm always happy to help." She tried to hide her smile as he raised his eyebrows at her formal response.

"Nada, how many times have I told you to call me Zack?" Actually his name was Zachary, but no one ever called him that.

She blushed, "I lost count, Dr. Thorton."

Zack laughed and shook his head. "Are you going to call me that at the party?"

Nada shook her head. "Only at work, Dr. Thorton." She already knew he would be at the party on Friday, since Mia couldn't wait to tell her. Everyone knew that Zack liked Nada and couldn't understand why she wouldn't go out with him. Nada did like the doctor, but she didn't date anyone. She didn't even have close friends, since she didn't know how she could ever explain who or what she was. She led a very private existence and hoped she could continue to do so.

"OK, I guess I'll leave it at that. I'll see you tomorrow." He winked at her before turning and heading back to the ER. Nada looked at the clock. Her replacement would be there any minute. As if on cue, Monica rounded the corner from the parking lot.

"I'm here, I'm here," she called as she approached. She also looked at the clock. "See, I have one minute to spare." She giggled as she headed for the employee lounge to put her purse in her locker. Nada shook her head, knowing the younger woman would take a smoke break before relieving her.

Fifteen minutes later, Nada unlocked her car and slid inside. She drove home quickly and let herself into her apartment. She threw her keys on the table next to the door and headed for the kitchen. After placing her purse on the counter, she took out the pint of blood. Before she left work, she took one of the donor pints from the laboratory fridge. She drained it into a resealable bag she brought with her, and thrown the original bag away. She made a notation on the chart that the blood had been contaminated and disposed of.

She put the bag into her own refrigerator and pulled out the container she didn't drink from that afternoon. She took off the top and stared at the thick red liquid. It wasn't at all tempting when it was cold, and she could only wish it weren't tempting when it was warm. Knowing that she needed it, she placed the container into the microwave to heat. As she stared at the container circling the inside of the machine, she thought about the party. Friday was only a day away, and Nada didn't really feel like being around a lot of people, but Mia pleaded. Nada never did anything with her co-workers, and they were beginning to wonder if something was wrong with her, or if she thought something was wrong with them. She wanted to get along with the people she worked with, so she knew she couldn't keep turning down their invitations. Mary, the head nurse, was retiring and the party was her send-off.

Nada knew she had nothing really to fear. The full moon was behind her that month, and she wouldn't have to worry about the next one for thirty days. Except for that one day a month, she could always control herself. As long as she had her daily ration of blood before the party, she wouldn't have to worry about that either. She had nothing to fear, she told herself again.

The microwave beeped, and she retrieved the container. She tested the temperature by sticking her index finger into the blood. After all the times she'd heated up the liquid in the past, she knew exactly how long it took to get it just right. Of course, she would prefer getting the blood fresh, but she would never take it from an unwilling person. Not to mention how much trouble she could get into. Nada put her finger into her mouth and closed her lips around it. As her tongue touched the warm wetness, her eyes closed with a sigh. As soon as she discovered she needed blood to survive, she had read every vampire book she could get her hands on. Since only a few of the myths applied to her and she also had werewolf tendencies, she didn't know what she was and didn't know whom to ask. If only she could remember what had made her so different. Nada knew she hadn't always been like this.  Every once in a while, she had memory flashes of years before. She knew she lost her parents at a young age, and a foster family raised her. They never cared about her though, so she left as soon as she turned eighteen. She had her birth certificate, driver's license and a passport, so she knew she was twenty-nine years old. She vaguely remembered backpacking across Europe several years earlier, but she couldn't recall details. Since that was about the time she *changed* for the first time, she knew something must have happened to her in one of those countries.

She drank the blood down with a few swallows and sighed as its warmth spread through her.  She closed her eyes for a moment and felt her headache fade. That was the first symptom that she needed blood. From past experience, she knew all the symptoms. If she didn't consume at least a cup of blood a day, she would get body aches all over that started in her head. She would then go very pale and clammy, and the shakes would start soon after. Her body hadn't let it get any further. Her subconscious took over at that point and she *changed*. What she *changed* into had then taken care of what she needed, and she made her first kill. Of course, it took several months before Nada remembered what she did when she *changed*, since she could recall most of what she did on nights other than ones with a full moon. It had been quite a shock to realize they hadn't been dreams. Recently, she acquired awareness of her surroundings during her *changes*, which was very bizarre and most unwelcome.

Nada rinsed the glass and filled it with water. She drank it and then placed the empty glass in the dishwasher. She could then decide what she wanted for dinner. Not wanting to cook anything, she pulled a microwavable dinner out of the freezer and heated it up. Nothing was wrong with her appetite. Other than the blood, she consumed what any other person would. She didn't think the blood was in any way nutritional for her. She had done some research on blood diseases and had come to the conclusion that her blood had something missing, and the only way to replenish what it needed was to consume blood. The only thing wrong with that theory was that her body wasn't particular about what kind of blood, since she drank animal blood quite often. Though, she realized that had some major side effects.

Nada didn't want to think about it anymore. She pulled her dinner out of the microwave, grabbed a fork, and left the kitchen. She walked into the living room and sat on the couch. Picking up the remote, she turned on the TV to watch the late news. When nothing out of the ordinary was reported, she sighed her relief. If she did something horrible during the full moon, she surely would have heard about it during her shift at the hospital. When the news ended at midnight, she flipped to her one premium channel. Putting the remote back on the coffee table, she settled in to watch and eat her dinner.

Nada awoke the next morning at around ten. She ate breakfast and watched the news. She had never killed a human before, but it always terrified her that she might during the full moon. She could only hope that her conscience stayed with her after she *changed*, and that she only fed upon the animals. So far, no human had been found drained of blood. She couldn't even be sure if the animals had been found, since their deaths weren't news worthy.

Not having to go to work, Nada turned on the radio. As she listened to the music, she sat on the floor and did stretching exercises. With her legs spread wide, she leaned forward until her chest touched the floor. Nada stretched her arms out above her head and let her fingers sift through the carpet fibers, sighing as she felt her muscles stretch. After a few moments, she pushed forward into a split and then rotated her hips into a side split. She leaned forward and touched her face to her right knee. She then stood and did a back bend. After flexing into the move at every possible angle, she kicked her legs over and somersaulted to a standing position. Nada then rolled her head from one side to the other. When she felt warmed up, she went out for her daily jog. She loved to run through the park, where she could watch all the people going about their lives. She watched them as she ran by, wishing she could be like them. Nada liked to run into the woods, where she could test her endurance levels. She ran as fast as she could, sometimes surprising the animals as she raced by. She enjoyed that the most, since it was as close to flying as any human could do on his or her own. Sometimes, she rested by lying in the leaves on the ground and staring up at the trees. If she were really quiet, some of the wildlife would wander by. Of course, they wouldn't come too close, as if sensing she was a danger to them.

When Nada finally got back to her apartment, her cheeks were flushed from the exertion of her long run. She immediately drank another cupful of blood, since one was never enough to sustain her all day after such an intense workout. After the blood, she drank an entire glass of water. She refilled the glass and slowly sipped the contents as she walked around her living room.

Her gaze moved to the easel next to the window. It had been awhile since she had last drawn, and the unfinished sketch cried out for completion. Nada walked closer and stared at the park scene. Since she ran among those trees so often, she had sketched the scene from memory. What she drew was very detailed. A little girl flew a kite, while her parents watched from their blanket and picnic lunch. A bird built a nest on a limb in a nearby tree, and a young couple embraced on a bench. As Nada's gaze went from crisp lines to smudged shadings, she shook her head. She didn't even know if she had studied or the drawing came naturally. Just another thing from her past that she couldn't remember. She only knew that drawing was one of her few escapes. Unfortunately, she hadn't had much time for escapes lately, at least when she was awake.

Nada sighed as she finished the last of the water and put the glass in the dishwater. She then took a long bath, letting the warm water soothe her overworked muscles. She smiled as she closed her eyes and leaned her head back. Nada would never understand why some people did not like to run. How else could they feel so alive?

When Nada got out of the tub, she lay back on her bed and stared at the ceiling. She had a few hours before she had to start getting ready for the party, and she enjoyed being able to slip away into her dreams. As she stared at the poster of the one man that she knew was most like her; she fantasized being enveloped by those strong arms. It didn't matter that he wasn't real, since she shouldn't be either. Nada closed her eyes and sighed, taking her fantasy with her as she fell asleep.

She was familiar with the dream, since she had it quite often. She and her vampire sat on a dock by a lake. He was still dressed in black, and now so was she. They were quite the couple sitting there, their heads so close together it was hard to see where one ended and the other began. His lips skimmed her neck, and Nada looked over his shoulder. Her brow furrowed when she saw the mountains. They had never been in the dream before.

She looked back at the man of her dreams to ask him about it, but she gasped. His face had changed to his vampiric facade, fangs and all.

"What's wrong?" She asked him. She would have said more, but his hand moved around her throat as he tilted her head to the side. She moved her hands up to his chest and shook her head. "Wait! What are you doing?"

His fingers squeezed her throat, and the pain surprised her. As her face began to *change*, she felt her teeth begin to sharpen. Nada ran her tongue over the sharp edges and cringed. "No!" She hissed at him.

He ignored her and moved in to strike. She finally made use of her hands on his chest and pushed. She didn't expect it to work and fell backwards into the lake.

Nada awoke with a start. Her eyes locked with the man on the poster above her, but she abruptly looked away. Her first impulse was to rip it down, but she sat up and took deep breaths. He was actually going to bite her, and that had never happened before. And what was with those mountains?

Doctor Grady Duncan loved animals. He had volunteered many hours during his career to stop animal abuse. He constantly gave free care at his month old veterinarian clinic, and he had several pets. What he currently stared at disturbed him greatly.

"Where did you say you found him?" Grady asked the man across from him.

"In the park. Have you ever seen anything like that before, Doc?" The man asked quickly.

Grady paused to look at the animal again. The dead fox had a vicious neck wound, but there was little blood. "Not really, but I'll have to examine him before I can know more." He looked up at the man. "Thank you for bringing him in."

"No problem. I'm just sorry you couldn't do anything for him. I know how you feel about these little guys."

Grady looked at the animal for a moment before responding. The fox had been dead for at least 24 hours, so he couldn't have done anything. It was also obvious that a few of the park animals had taken advantage of an easy meal. Grady bit his lip in thought.

"Thanks again, Fred." He didn't look up as he spoke, unable to tear his eyes away from the fox. He never saw one up close before. Alive, it must have been a beautiful animal.

Fred backed out of the office. "I'll see you later, Doc. Maybe I can find you a live one next time." He waved and was gone.

Grady finally looked up and watched his retreating back. He then turned his attention back to the fox.

An hour later he sat at his desk, transcribing his notes from the autopsy. The obvious cause of death was blood loss from the neck wound. All the other gashes had occurred after death by different animals, which was common due to the length of time the body had been in the park. Since no blood marred the animal's fur, it looked as if it had been drained of blood. Going by the teeth marks, a much larger animal killed the fox. Grady found that very strange. It was the third case he'd seen in the last month. He wondered if that's all there were, or if those were the only ones turned into him?

Grady pulled out the folder where he kept the unexplained deaths. He took pictures of all three animals. The two pictures currently in the folder were of a cat and an owl. Both animals died of blood loss from a neck wound, and the owl had nearly been beheaded. If these had been humans, the police would be involved, but Grady knew they wouldn't care about these "murders." He did think of them as murders, and he wished he knew how to find their killer. Any animal that would do this needed to be put down, but he couldn't think of too many animals that only drank the blood from their victims.

"What the hell is that?" A voice asked right at his ear. Grady jumped so violently that the top of his head struck the chin of the man above him. He jumped up and spun around.

"Damn it, Kiefer! Don't sneak up on me like that!" He yelled at his friend and put the file away.

Kiefer rubbed his chin and winced. "I'll take that under advisement. Christ, Grady, why so nervous?"

Grady stood and put his hand on his head. "I guess that teaches me for not locking the front door.

Damn, couldn't you have let me know you were in the room?"

Kiefer grinned and pulled a six-pack of beer from a brown paper bag. "Didn't think you'd be working on top secret stuff, pal. What is so important that you'd still be working on it this late? I couldn't believe your light was still on. I was on my way to the club down the street when I saw your car." He pulled one of the cans free and tossed it to Grady.

Grady caught it and glared at his friend. He took a deep breath and closed his eyes as he popped the top of the can. As he drank deeply, he sighed. "I guess I *did* need a break." He opened his eyes and watched his friend open his own beer and take a drink. He met Kiefer shortly after moving to LA, since they lived in the same apartment complex. He worked as a physical therapist and had his own clinic, so he helped Grady secure the suite next door.

"Come on, you don't really want to waste a whole Friday night looking at animals, do you? Didn't you tell me that you wanted to try that club?" He held up the beer can and shook it.

Grady stood abruptly and grabbed his jacket. "You're right. I do need a break."

# Chapter Three

Nada sat at a corner table with four others. Three were her co-workers, Mia, Dr. Zachary Thorton and Monica, and the fourth person was Mia's boyfriend, Jamal. Zack sat next to Nada. He just bought a round of drinks and convinced her to try a rum and coke. She didn't like to drink liquor, since she preferred to be alert at all times. Still being a little shook up from her dream, Nada decided to tempt fate a little. She slowly sipped the drink, surprised that it did taste pretty good.

Mary, the guest of honor, gyrated on the dance floor with one of the other doctors. They were both drunk and attempting to do the Electric Slide. Zack asked Nada if she wanted to try the dance, but Nada shook her head. He shrugged and ran out onto the dance floor. Soon, everyone was out there, and Nada sat alone at the table. She didn't remember ever seeing the line dance before, but it looked fun. Mary kept stepping on Zack's feet, and everyone laughed. Nada smiled at their camaraderie, suddenly feeling very out of place. Zack motioned for her to join them, but she ignored him. She wanted to participate, but she also feared it. She avoided groups of people for a reason, especially people engaged in a physical activity. Their bodies heated up, which made their hearts pump faster, until she could almost hear the blood rushing through their veins. At times like those she lost a bit of herself, and she didn't like feeling that way. It made it harder to convince herself that she was still human. She didn't like feeling as if she were a predator among her prey.

Nada looked away and ran her hands over her face. She broke out in a sweat and glanced over at her drink to discover it was nearly empty. She knew she didn't want to drink alcohol. She always had to stay levelheaded, but her common sense lapsed for a few minutes. She forgot she couldn't enjoy certain things that normal people took for granted. Nada suddenly needed fresh air, so she got up and headed for the side door that led to the patio.

She walked over to the railing, which overlooked the ocean. A gentle breeze caressed her flushed cheeks. She took a deep breath and sighed. A waitress walked over to ask if she needed anything, and she requested water. Nada watched her walk away, but a man stopped the waitress to order a beer. Nada's gaze lingered on him. His hair was a darker shade of brown than hers and was as wavy as hers was straight. She guessed that he probably had to blow dry his hair to keep it from being curly, which would also explain why he kept it so short.

Nada's gaze finally lowered to his face. By this time he must have sensed her watching, since he turned to look at her. The outdoor lighting caused several shadows to spread across his clean-shaven face, but she could clearly see his dark green eyes. He looked tan, but Nada guessed that was due more to his parents than to the sun. He smiled at her, and she had a hard time holding back her own smile. He had one of those smiles that people say would light up a room. It also made him appear almost cherubic, if that was possible for a man older than her with such a dark complexion.

He unwound himself from the small chair and stood, and she noticed his height put him at least a foot taller than she. When it looked as if he would approach her, she set her mouth in a firm line, shook her head and turned back to the railing. She stood there until she sensed him walk the other direction. Turning to look, she watched his retreating back as he walked to the far side of the patio. Nada felt a twinge of regret, but she knew it couldn't go anywhere. She didn't like how she immediately felt she could trust him. How could she trust a man she had never met? She wasn't out to make any new friends. She had a hard enough time being friendly with the people she worked with.

Grady sat at one of the patio tables in the corner and looked at the small brunette at the railing. She had looked so friendly until he had approached. She had almost looked afraid of the prospect of him getting close to her, and he couldn't even blame it on Kiefer. His friend had found a sexy blonde to dance with, so Grady had retreated to the patio. He decided he preferred to sit by himself and nurse a beer, until the small brunette stepped through the door. He watched the wind blowing through her long, thick hair. She closed her eyes and leaned her head back. He looked from her bare throat down to her modest outfit. She wore a black shirt, black jeans and black boots. She had a nice body, he admitted, more athletic than voluptuous with everything proportioned well. When she gripped the railing, Grady could see her arm muscles flex. He frowned as he realized she kept gripping the railing and wondered what made her so tense. She finally turned away from the railing and their gazes locked. Grady didn't dare blink or move; afraid she would bolt if he did either. As they stared at each other, Grady had the distinct impression of a deer being caught in headlights. That expression shown clearly in her eyes.

The waitress broke the trance. She handed the water to Nada, who tore her gaze from Grady.

"Thank you." She pulled a dollar out of her pocket and handed it to the girl. The waitress smiled her thanks before heading over to Grady to give him the beer he ordered. Grady had to look away from Nada while he looked in his wallet for money. After he paid for his beer, he looked back to see that Nada had gone.

Nada left the party without saying anything to her colleagues. She'd been tempted to find Mia but knew the younger woman would not let her leave. Nada didn't want the conflict, so she just left. Not wanting to go home, she drove to the park, which strangely always felt like home to her. Of course, she didn't like waking up naked in it, but that rarely happened. She sat on a bench and took a deep breath.

Her thoughts returned to the man in the bar, and she exhaled a shaky breath. It was strange how he made her feel. They hadn't even spoken, but their locked gazes spoke volumes. Nada never experienced that with anyone before. At least she didn't remember such an occasion. She almost regretted leaving the club, since she would probably never see him again. It troubled her that she didn't even know his name.

The next day at work, Nada caught hell for leaving the club. She apologized by saying she hadn't felt well and didn't wanted to ruin anyone else's evening. Mia shrugged and gave her a knowing look. Nada bit her lip, wondering if she had blown her chance to bond with her co-workers. Mia caught her expression and quickly told her not to worry about it, and that there would be other parties.

Nada tried not to cringe and smiled instead. "I know, but I'm sorry I was inconsiderate. I don't want you to think I don't appreciate being included. I'm just so used to being on my own." She finished with a shrug.

Mia placed a hand on her shoulder and shook her head. "That's not healthy, honey. You're too pretty to be alone." She winked. "Ya need some churn in your life. That won't be too easy sans man, ya know?"

Nada chuckled. Mia had her own language and used it on occasion. It never failed to make her laugh. "I'm not in a rush to have *children*, Mia, but I do want them someday." It surprised Nada to have her thoughts return to the man from the club. As she pictured them doing what made children, she blushed. "And I would prefer to have them *with* a man than without." She squeezed Mia's hand and laughed again.

The rest of the weekend went by quickly and uneventfully. When Nada got home Sunday night, it was actually Monday morning. Her hospital shift turned into a double and dawn would quickly approach. Most people would be getting up for work, and she was just about to go to bed. Nada yawned as she walked through her apartment, placing her purse on the kitchen counter as she passed by. She rubbed her eyes as she walked into her bedroom. Taking off her uniform, she pulled on her nightshirt.

She stood in the middle of her bedroom trying to remember what she needed to do, but her mind was blank. Being too tired to brush her teeth, she went to bed.

Nada couldn't sleep as late as she would have liked. A headache woke her, and she suddenly remembered what she forgot to do before going to bed. She threw back the covers and ran for the kitchen. Her purse sat on the counter with the blood still inside. She groaned as she pulled out the bag, which she how somehow forgotten to put in the refrigerator. It was as if she hadn't been doing the same thing for years. Nada wondered what eight hours of room temperature would do to blood, as she opened the bag and tentatively sniffed the contents. She hissed and pulled back, covering her mouth. She didn't even know she *could* hiss. The image of a cat crossed her mind, and she lost hold of the bag. It hit the floor at her feet, and the thick blood splattered everywhere. Nada jumped up and landed on the counter in a crouch. She arched her back and noticed she could no longer focus on her hands.

She ran through the park, and an animal chased her. It seemed familiar to her, but she couldn't grasp its name at that moment. Being too afraid of it to think straight, she tried to run faster so she could make it to the tree. She was almost there, when it lunged at her. A terrible pain coursed through her as it bit into her back. She screamed, but a hiss came out instead. The pain was excruciating, and she fought to stay conscious. As everything grew dark, she heard a man yell and a dog yelp. That's what it had been, a dog. Then all went black.

Grady sat at his desk, when Fred ran in carrying something in a bloody towel.

"I got here as fast as I could, Doc. This one's still alive. I had to beat the damn dog off of it though."

Grady pushed out of his chair in an instant, and he directed Fred toward the operating table. When Fred placed his bundle on the table, Grady put his hand over it. He called for his assistant, Margaret, who ran in a moment later. She helped him hold the animal as they took off the towel.

The animal lying inside surprised him, since he'd never before seen such a large cat. It amazed him that a dog even attempted to attack it and concluded the canine must be rabid. Had it been responsible for the dead animals found recently? "What kind of dog was it?"

"Hell, I don't know. It looked like a mix between a pit bull and a rottweiler."

"Was it rabid?"

"I didn't ask it, Doc," he chuckled, "but I had to beat it senseless before it would back off."

Grady looked at Margaret. "Might want to call that in. We can't have a rabid animal running around the park."

She nodded and left the room. Grady turned to Fred. "Thanks for bringing her in, Fred," he said as he looked at the cat's dark brown fur. Of course, it looked nearly auburn with the blood mixed in. He had to operate immediately, or she'd die. "I'm going to have to ask you to leave, Fred. I need to get her stitched up."

"Sure thing, Doc." Fred backed up, reluctant to leave. Grady looked at him and nodded. Fred nodded and then left. Grady's gaze returned to the cat, and he stroked her side. Her eyes opened, and they locked on him.

"Don't worry, love, I'll have you fixed up in no time." He reached for the razor to shave the wounded area and walked around to the other side of the table. Just as he placed the razor to the fur, he could no longer focus on her. Grady put the razor down and rubbed his eyes. When he looked again, he realized there was nothing wrong with his eyes.

Grady watched in shock as the fur disappeared into the skin, and the body stretched. As the legs and forearms lengthened, he took a step back. He couldn't take his eyes off the animal on the table and watched as the skull enlarged and reshaped itself into human size. The fur on her head changed to human hair and lengthened until it fell over the side of the table like a curtain. He watched as the wound in her back healed in front of his eyes. Grady jumped back about a foot as she pushed up to her hands and knees and turned to look at him.

"Oh my, God!" He breathed. As her features cleared, and he focused on her face, he gasped. She was the woman from the nightclub. Their gazes locked for mere seconds, before she looked away. Grady's gaze traveled down her body. Her arms blocked her breasts from view, but he had been right about her being athletic. Every muscle in her trim body was flexed.

Grady's mouth fell open as the woman blurred again. This time feathers protruded all over her body as it shrunk. Her legs shortened and thinned. Her arms flattened and lengthened into wings. It was like watching a computer morph a picture of a human into one of a bird, though he never thought he'd actually witness it in the flesh. A few moments later, he stared at a large owl.

"Oh my, God!" He repeated slowly. She spread her wings and started flapping them. Soon she flew around the large room, looking for an exit. Grady didn't know what to do. He watched her circle the room a few times and winced at her shrill cries. Against his better judgment, he walked to the window. The owl looked at him and flew closer. He unlocked the window and pushed it open, and she flew out without a backward glance. He watched until he could no longer see her.

It took several minutes before he was able to snap out of his shock. He ran across the room and grabbed his keys.

Nada headed to the park. She hadn't wanted to *change* in front of him, but she couldn't wait any longer. She had lost too much blood and needed to feed, but she had to get away from him. She then pictured an animal that could fly.

As soon as Nada arrived in the park, she landed on a low branch. She looked around to make sure no one could see her, before she *changed* again. She thought of an animal more aggressive than a cat.

A few minutes later, a wolf jumped down from the branch. She licked her lips and scanned her surroundings.

When Nada awoke, she lay naked in front of her coffee table. Her headache had gone, but she had other things to worry about. She recognized the man from the party Friday night, and he had definitely recognized her. She never *changed* in front of a human before, but she didn't have a choice. She could feel herself dying and knew that he would not have been able to save the cat.

Needing to decide what to do about him, Nada took a few deep breaths and forced herself to concentrate. Luckily, he hadn't seen her with her friends. He didn't know anything about her, but it served her right for going out at all. Though it didn't matter as much that he recognized her, but that he saw her *change*, not once but twice. She suddenly remembered that he opened the window for her. He didn't have to do that, and she wondered why he had. He could have attempted to capture her instead. She then remembered feeling as if she could trust him when she first saw him Friday night. Maybe that feeling was justified. She always wished for someone to talk to about her *situation*. Could she trust him enough to see him again? Nada thought about that for a moment and decided she did want to see him again.

She looked at the clock, which read 5:00 p.m. Four hours had passed. She stood and walked to the kitchen, which still had blood all over it. She opened the cabinet and pulled out the ammonia and bucket. The congealed blood took quite a while to clean up.  Since she fed earlier, she had no problem disposing of it. She would definitely need to be more careful in the future.

## Chapter Four

Grady drove up every street in the neighborhood and even walked through the park, but he didn't find the owl. When he finally got back into his car, he realized how stupid he'd been. If she could morph from a cat to a human to an owl, she could probably turn into other animals as well. He doubted she stayed an owl for long. He would probably never see her again.

He walked back into his clinic and brushed off Margaret, as she opened her mouth to speak.

"But, sir..."

Grady closed his office door behind him, cutting her off. When he saw who stood in his office, he nearly fell back against the closed door. He turned around and opened it a crack. "Thanks for holding down the fort, Margaret. You can go ahead and leave if you'd like."

She looked at the clock. It wasn't even 7:00, and she usually didn't leave work until 8:00 but went to collect her things.

Grady closed the door and turned back to the woman. She had been sitting but now stood to the side of the chair. She looked afraid of him, and he held up his hands.

"I'm not going to hurt you," he tried to reassure her. He forgot how beautiful she was, and his eyes took in her appearance in seconds. She wore a large white shirt and brown shorts with sneakers. The nondescript outfit hid what a nice figure she had, but nothing could take away from her ethereal face.

She recognized his voice and smiled. *Don't worry, love, I'll have you fixed up in no time,* he had told her. She looked around the office, and her gaze settled on the other door. As she walked into the operating room, Grady followed silently. She stopped by the table and placed her hands on it.

"Thank you," she told him without looking at him. It still amazed her that she had the courage to face him and hoped she wasn't making a mistake.

Hearing her voice for the first time made her more real to Grady. Without thinking he walked over to her and touched her arm, surprised when she didn't flinch. She felt like any other warm-blooded woman he had ever touched. "You're welcome," he replied.

She turned toward him, and he looked into her eyes. They were dark brown, like her hair. His gaze fell on her long mane, and he reached out and touched a few strands. It felt like human hair.

"Can I see your back?" He asked it before he thought. He almost wished he could take it back, but she shrugged and turned around. She pulled the shirt over her head, and he discovered with surprise that she wore nothing beneath it. She clutched her shirt in her hands and exposed her entire back to him. He looked at it for a moment before reaching out a hand to touch. His fingers traced an area where the wound should be, but he couldn't even see a scar. He realized his eyes hadn't been playing tricks on him. Grady withdrew his hand but kept staring at where the wound should have been.

"Can I put my shirt back on now?" She asked in her silky smooth voice.

Grady snapped to attention and nodded but then realized she couldn't see him. "Yes, I'm sorry."

She turned around. "No need," she replied as she pulled the shirt back on. He couldn't keep from looking at her breasts before the shirt covered them. Only two things could have caused her nipples to harden. He doubted the reason could be excitement and looked at her arms. Chill bumps covered both of them. He asked her to take off her shirt in a cold lab. Feeling guilty, Grady reached for her wrist and rubbed his own hand down her arm. As he repeated the process on her other arm, he drew in his breath. He didn't even know the woman, and he rubbed her arms? Grady let go of her wrist and looked at her face. He opened his mouth to apologize but then saw her expression. He could only compare it to when he scratched his cats behind their ears. His touch must have been soothing.

"What's your name?" He asked as he shook his head. Her closed eyes slowly opened.

"Nada," she quietly replied. "Spelled like nah-da but pronounced nay-da." She added in a clearly automated response. She blushed prettily. "Sorry...habit."

Grady fought the chuckle at her cuteness. "Nada what?" he asked.

She breathed deeply and passed him on her way back to his office. He again followed silently and watched how gracefully she walked. She made no sound as she moved. She sat in one of his chairs and crossed her legs. As Grady watched her do such a completely normal thing, he almost forgot that normal didn't apply to her.

"I'd prefer to stay on a first name basis, if you don't mind," Nada replied, running her right hand down her left arm. She enjoyed his touch and wondered why he had stopped so suddenly. She couldn't even remember a time when anyone, let alone a man, had touched her so much. That he didn't seem to be afraid of her pleased her the most. After what he had witnessed earlier, she had expected the worst when he stepped into his office and saw her standing there. She stared into his eyes, resisting the desire to place his hands back on her arms. He was even better looking than she remembered.

"What? Oh, of course, I understand." Grady walked around his desk and sat down. He leaned back in his chair and rubbed his chin with the back of his left hand. He then stretched and scratched the back of his head as he stared at her. "What can I do for you, Nada?" He finally asked her.

She took another deep breath and licked her dry lips, suddenly very nervous. She had never spoken about herself to anyone. Her gaze fell to the nameplate on his desk. "Can I trust you, Doctor Duncan?"

"Oh, please, call me Grady, and yes, I think you can trust me."

It wasn't exactly the answer she wanted, but it would do. "I need help, Grady."

"Yes, I think you do," he replied, unable to look away from her. He loved animals and always helped them when he could. He knew instinctively that an animal in need sat across from him. "Why don't you start at the beginning?" He suggested.

Her brows arched as she frowned. "At the beginning?" Nada paused to think and slowly shook her head. "I don't know the beginning." As tears unexpectedly filled her eyes, she closed them and took a few deep breaths. Nada slid from the chair to sit on the floor, pulling her knees up to her chest and circling them with her arms.

Grady leaned forward in surprise. He watched her rock forward and back, before leaving his chair and coming around the desk to kneel on the floor in front of her.

"Then just start wherever you want to." He touched her knee. Her cheek moved against it, and she sighed.

Nada hadn't realized how much she missed human contact. Since she just fed, she didn't worry that his nearness might set her off. Her human side begged for this closeness, and she gave into it.

"I've never talked about it. Why don't you just ask questions, and I'll answer if I can?" Nada suggested, still pressing her cheek against his hand.

Grady didn't know how to feel, but he knew he didn't want to move his hand. He smiled as a ridiculous question came to mind. He knew he shouldn't but asked it anyway. "Are you a vampire?" She couldn't be responsible for the animals that had been drained of blood, could she? Even as he asked it, he realized that she could be.

She looked up, and their gazes locked. Being so close to him, she could tell his eyes weren't dark green as she had first thought. They were more of a hazel green. As she stared at all the vibrant colors, she thought about what he had asked. She smiled at such an obvious question. "You don't believe in those, do you?"

"Well, several bodies have been found recently that were drained of blood."

Nada's eyes widened, and she gasped. "What kind of bodies?"

Grady realized he hadn't been specific, and he reached out to place his hands on her shoulders. "Animals, Nada. I'm not talking about people."

She relaxed under his hands and sighed. "No, of course not. Only vampires kill people that way." She got a faraway look in her eyes. "I've read up on them, you know? Ever since I discovered I was different, I have tried to find out what I am." She paused and tried to control the tears that threatened to fall. "Vampires are fantasy. You can only kill them with stakes through the heart or chopping off their heads. They don't like garlic or sunlight, and they sleep in coffins. They turn into bats and miraculously turn back to human shape fully clothed." She scoffed at that before continuing. "Are their clothes in suspended animation while they're bats? Anyway, I can go on, but I only have a few things in common with them. I don't like the sunlight, but it won't kill me. It hurts my eyes, but I'm fine with sunglasses. The main thing is that I need blood to survive. I don't have fangs, at least in human form. I don't sleep in a coffin, and I *like* garlic. I have a pulse, for Christ's sake. I'm not dead, or undead, whichever the case may be." She gave up on holding back the tears, and they ran unchecked down her cheeks. "I can't even change into a bat, but only because I've never killed one." She tried to make it sound funny but failed miserably. That realization just depressed her more, and she leaned forward. As years of pent-up feelings finally released, her small form racked with sobs. She hadn't realized how hard it would be to talk about it.

She shocked Grady speechless, and the top of her head pressed against his chest. Not knowing what else to do, he lifted a hand and stroked her back. When that seemed to calm her, he raised the other hand to the back of her head and stroked her hair. He hoped she wasn't responsible for draining the blood from those animals, but she had just admitted to needing blood. Maybe the vampire myths were ridiculous, but what would a real life vampire be like?

"Can you only be killed with a stake through the heart?" He asked, half-joking and half dead serious. He could still visualize the wound in her back healing itself.

Nada felt his touch all through her body. Her tears stopped, and she pressed herself closer to his warmth. His arms encircled her as she moved her body against his. She nuzzled his neck. "You smell good," she muttered and kissed his jaw. She felt him tense and suddenly realized what she was doing.

Grady almost yelled at her quick response. She pushed away from him and sat in the chair before he could even blink. He stood almost as quickly and fell against his desk. "What the hell just happened?"

Nada held up a hand and shook her head. "I don't want to even think about it." She couldn't remember a time when she got that close to any man. The need to be one with him was too strong, as well as the unexpected surge of sexual emotions that flowed through her.

"What do you mean?"

She finally met his gaze. "Didn't you feel it?" She asked him. "You must have, or you wouldn't have reacted like that." She accused him with her eyes.

At first he didn't realize what she meant, but then it became clearer. After discussing vampires and thinking of those animals drained of blood, she nuzzled his neck. He tensed on impulse, but he didn't think she meant that. What could he have felt, besides a beautiful woman kissing him? If she had been an ordinary woman, he might even have been turned on. He definitely felt attracted to her.

"Well, damn it, Nada, *should* I be afraid of you?" He reached for the folder of the three dead animals and handed her the pictures. "Are you responsible for this?"

Nada looked at all three of the pictures without showing any emotion. It relieved her to know that he tensed out of fear and not because he felt her attraction. She reminded herself that her senses were much better than his. She finally looked at him as she handed the pictures back to him. "Tomorrow, you'll have another to add to your list."

Grady took the pictures from her and walked around the desk to his chair. He had his "killer," but what would he do about it? He remembered her strong reaction when he mentioned the bodies being found drained of blood. If she knew she killed them, why had she been surprised? He reassured her they weren't human, and she calmed down. Wouldn't she know that she hadn't killed a human? Something didn't feel right, but he didn't know what it could be. He looked toward the lab as he tried to sort through all the information he'd been given. "What did you turn into after you flew out of here?" He sat down and put the pictures back in the folder.

"A wolf."

"A wolf?" The park didn't have any wolves, and it had been daylight outside when she left the clinic. "Why a wolf? You're lucky someone didn't shoot you." He doubted Fred would bring in a wounded wolf.

"I had lost too much blood. My body chose the wolf, since I needed an aggressive hunter that could get me as much blood as possible. I made a mistake with the cat and hope not to repeat it. I had been feeding on a rat, when the dog attacked me."

Grady almost didn't want to know but asked anyway, "What animal did you feed on as a wolf?"

She looked down to her lap. "The dog that attacked me."

"It could have been rabid!" He replied, in shock.

"It wasn't. It was just hungry, and I put it out of its misery."

Grady stared at the phone for a moment. He knew he should report her, but shouldn't she be more important than a few dead animals? He sensed she was an animal as well. If that were true, he owed her every chance to survive. "Can your body only repair itself when you *morph?*" He asked, knowing the answer.

"Well, my regenerative abilities are advanced, but it's quicker if I..." she paused and smiled. She had never used his term before. *"Morph,"* she finished without breaking eye contact.

He nodded and thought back to Friday night. He remembered feeling as if she had been caught in the glare of headlights. It felt strange to have related her to an animal before he knew anything about her. He realized she never answered his earlier question about dying by a stake through the heart. He decided to reword it. "Can you be killed?"

"If the trauma is severe enough," she nodded, wondering if he asked out of curiosity or self-preservation. He didn't seem afraid of her, but could she be completely sure? He *had* tensed when she got too close. "I doubt I could regenerate a new head."

Grady couldn't help but smile at that. "How long have you been like this?"

She shrugged. "Less than three years."

That surprised him. He had thought she would either have no idea or say her entire life. "What made you like this?"

She shrugged again. "I don't know."

"You don't know?" He asked with doubt in his tone.

Nada's eyebrows shot up, and she cocked her head to the side. "I don't know," she repeated. "I have no memory of what made me like this. All I know is that I haven't always been this way."

Grady thought about that for a moment. "How do you know *that*?"

Nada closed her eyes as she tried to pull from her memories. The images were never clear, but she knew she had human parents. Even though she couldn't picture her friends' faces, she knew she grew up with them.

Grady searched her face and then let his gaze travel down her body, noticing her hands clenched into fists. He looked back at her face to see that she had opened her eyes.  Her steady gaze returned his stare. "Nada?"

"Would you like to see my birth certificate? My driver's license? My passport? I don't have any pictures of my family, though I could probably dig up my senior yearbook.  My parents died a long time ago, and I guess no one thought it important enough for me to have pictures of them. I certainly don't remember ever being tempted to drink blood when I drank beer with my friends." She could have said more but knew he got the point. She crossed her arms under her breasts and sat back in the chair.

Grady could only stare at first. She spoke in a soft even voice, but he could see she was irritated. He certainly didn't know her well enough to call her a liar, but he felt tempted to say he *did* want to see her driver's license. "You have a passport?"

"I went to Europe three years ago." She replied with a nod.

"Why?"

"I don't know." She replied slowly, daring him to repeat it again.

Grady smiled at the defiant look in her eyes. "Did you go alone, or is that another 'I don't know'?"

Her eyebrows went up. "All I know is that I came back by myself."

"Have you ever been to a doctor?"

She shook her head. "I was too afraid of what they'd find."

He nodded. "If you'll let me draw blood, I can send it to the lab to be analyzed."

She shook her head. "What would you tell the technicians when they ask for an explanation?"

Grady opened his mouth to speak but paused. He didn't have an answer.

Nada shook her head again. "That's precisely why I won't go to the doctor."

He took a deep breath. "Why did you come back here tonight, Nada? What do you want from me?"

She looked into his eyes and thought about it. "Maybe I just needed someone to talk to."

"I'm a vet, not a shrink. Have you ever tried talking to one of them?"

Nada didn't bother shaking her head. "I could just imagine what one of them would do with me if they knew what you do. The only reason I'm here is because you saw me *change*, but you let me go." She stood and approached the desk. Placing her palms on the edge, she leaned forward. "Something in your eyes told me that I could trust you. I doubt I could so easily find that elsewhere. Am I wrong?"

Only a few inches separated their faces, and he looked into her dark brown eyes. He couldn't deny feeling drawn to her, and he realized he wanted to help her. He stared into her eyes for a moment longer before taking a deep breath. "I don't know."

A glimmer of a smile pierced her serious look.

# Chapter Five

When Nada got home, she felt pretty good. Grady had been a good listener and made her feel comfortable, and it felt wonderful to talk about her problems. Before she left, he gave her a business card with his home number written on the back. He told her to call any time she needed to talk. Having made her feel so comfortable, she knew he must be a great vet.

Nada left his clinic without giving him her last name or phone number. Her home was her sanctuary, and she had to be completely sure she could trust him before letting him know too much. She changed into her exercise clothes and went out.

She couldn't stop thinking about Grady as she ran. She'd only talked to him for about an hour before leaving his office, but she felt as if she'd known him much longer. It felt as if he'd always been in her life, and it certainly felt good to be able to think of having someone in her life. She'd been alone for a long time.

Nada stopped running as she realized he might have someone in his life already. They had only talked about her problems, and she hadn't even noticed whether he wore a wedding ring. She looked around and noticed an attractive couple sitting on a nearby bench. She watched them kiss. It wouldn't be fair to expect Grady to want a relationship with her. She didn't even think she could have a normal relationship with a man. She didn't know if she'd ever be able to lead a normal life, or even have children. She wanted children, so she tried not to think about the possibility of never having them. She shook her head and started running again.

The following morning, Grady sat at his desk. It disappointed him that Nada wouldn't let him take any of her blood, since he was curious to see if it matched the blood that had come out of her as a cat. After she flew out of the room, he ran for his keys. On his way out, he happened to look on the table and saw the bloody towel. He paused to stare at it for a moment, before putting it in a sterile bag and placing it in the mini-fridge he used to store specimens. He'd then run out to look for Nada. Right after she left his office as a woman, he retrieved the towel and sent a sample of the blood to his lab. He practiced what he would tell Kenny, the technician, when he called. Grady didn't have to wait very long as he reached for the phone.

"You've reached Dr. Duncan."

"Hey, Dr. D. I think there is a problem with the blood you sent over yesterday." Kenny announced.

"What do you mean?" Grady asked and held his breath.

"It must have been contaminated. I've never seen anything like it. What kind of animal did you get it from?" Kenny asked.

"A cat," Grady responded honestly.

"What kind of shape was it in? Did it look like it had been in several fights?"

Grady didn't like how Kenny referred to Nada as an *it*, but he held his tongue. Even if she had been just a cat, she wouldn't be an *it*. He cleared his throat. "She was in bad shape when she was brought in. A dog nearly killed her. What is wrong with the blood?"

Grady heard the shuffling of paper before Kenny spoke again. "Well, let's see, where should I start? First off, this blood looks like it came from numerous sources, almost like a blood cocktail." Kenny began.

"Numerous sources? Like what?" Grady pressed.

"Well, I can't give you an exact count, since that would take months of study, but what I did find before giving up is that the blood contains a few species of bird and a variety of small and medium sized mammals. What really threw me is that human blood is in it. But what's weirder than that is none of the species are distinct. They're merged, almost like they were spliced together, which makes it even harder to determine the species of animal." He paused again. "Now that you mention it being from a cat, that is the strongest presence in the blood. Human comes right after that. The third is unrecognizable, and all the others vary. I tell you Dr. D., this is the weirdest shit I've ever seen. Like I said, this would literally take months of research to sort out."

"What do you mean that the third is unrecognizable?" Grady asked.

"I mean that it is an uncharted DNA. I'm not even sure if it's bird or mammal, but since all the other animals are warm blooded, it must be, too. But like I said, the sample must have been contaminated with other blood. This is impossible."

Grady covered his mouth for a moment. *Uncharted DNA* echoed inside his head. The cat had been the strongest blood, since that's what Nada had been at the time. Of course human came next, but what about the third? Could it be what had changed her? Kenny's voice interrupted his thoughts.

"What do you want me to do with this sample, Doc?"

Grady sent the sample to the lab with a note that no one was to touch it except for Kenny. He trusted the young man, but would he be able to keep an uncharted DNA to himself, or would he really convince himself that the blood was contaminated? Grady gave free care to Kenny's dog soon after opening the clinic, so the young man felt indebted to him. Could that be enough to ensure silence? "Would you please send it and all copies of the findings back to me?" He didn't ask Kenny not to keep the original, but he knew the young man would understand what he asked of him.

"Sure thing, Doc. I'd actually like to get it away from me. It's a bit too *Twilight Zone* for me, if you know what I mean." He laughed, but Grady didn't join in.

"Yeah, I know what you mean. Thanks a lot, Kenny. I owe you one."

"Agh, don't worry about it, Doc. After what you did for Rosco, I'll always owe *you*. I'll talk to you later," and he hung up.

Grady stared at the phone for a moment before hanging it up, almost relieved that Nada didn't consent to giving away any of her blood. It would be harder to convince Kenny that he had somehow contaminated two different blood samples, not to mention that human would be the strongest presence in her blood, and the uncharted species would probably be second. He shivered, though not from being cold. Nada hadn't even told him everything about her situation, and that worried him the most. Of course, he didn't know that for sure, but he sensed she had held back. In a way he was glad, since he had enough to assimilate. He already had questions for their next meeting, and he hoped there would be a next one. She left him no way of contacting her, so he could only hope she would either call or stop by the clinic. He had a feeling she would do one or both, since she had no one else. He tried and failed to imagine the life she led.

# Chapter Six

The following night, Nada had trouble getting to sleep. She hugged her pillow and stared at the window. She couldn't get Grady out of her mind, something she had tried to do since their talk. The more she thought about him, the more she realized that she didn't know much about him. She felt as if she could trust him, but she didn't know that for sure. She knew that if she spent any more time with him that she might be tempted to reveal more about herself, and he already knew too much. He wanted her blood of all things. What would he do with the results if he had it?

With a groan, she rolled onto her back and looked up. Even though the room was dark, she could clearly see the ceiling. She fought her first impulse to look away. "Hey, Sexy," she whispered.

Nada had resisted the urge to take the poster down, and her dream lover still smiled down at her. He usually helped her get to sleep most nights, but she feared bringing him into her dreams since the last one and avoided even looking at the poster. Had that nightmare been just a fluke? She hated to admit that she missed him and watching the show wasn't enough. He was the closest thing she had to a boyfriend. She fastened her gaze on his shoulder, but she forced herself to look into his eyes. His sly smile made her lower lip tremble. Deciding he deserved one more chance, she sighed and began to visualize being in his arms. Before she knew it, she fell asleep.

She didn't let her guard down at first, expecting things to get bad. The appearance of the mountains again didn't immediately alarm her, especially since her vampire didn't get nasty as he had before. She sighed with contentment and closed her eyes. Her arms slowly moved around him, and her fingers caressed the muscles in his back.

*Γιατί ονειρεύεστε τον?*

Nada's eyes opened and her gaze darted around her surroundings. Except for the man kissing her neck, she saw no one else. She took another slow look around but still didn't see anyone. Hesitantly, she closed her eyes once again. She winced as she felt her upper arms gripped painfully.

*"Γιατί συνεχίζετε τον?"*

The voice hissed in the same strange language, but this time it began to sound familiar.

When Nada's eyes snapped open, her gaze locked on the face that should have been a certain famous vampire, but it began to *morph* into something else. The skin turned black, the face elongated and the eyes began to glow. His black trench coat *morphed* into a set of wings on his back.

"No!" She screamed and covered her face so she wouldn't have to see anymore of the horrible transformation.

When she moved her arms aside, Nada again stared at the poster above her bed. In one swift jump she tore it from the ceiling. As she landed on the floor beyond the foot of the bed, the crumpled poster headed for the trash can.

Though Nada couldn't keep Grady out her mind, she managed to wait a few more days before contacting him. Since she couldn't count on her dreams to comfort her, she needed to be around someone she trusted. She called him at home on Friday night.

Grady got back from walking his dog. He opened the back door and the greyhound bounded outside, where his food dish awaited him. Grady then walked to the kitchen to feed his cats. He had just filled the water dish, when the phone rang. He grabbed the kitchen extension. "Hello?"

"Doctor Duncan?" He heard after a slight pause.

Grady smiled upon recognizing her voice. He began to think he'd never hear from her. "Didn't I tell you to call me Grady?" He asked her.

There was another pause. "Sorry, Grady."

"No problem, Nada. It's good to hear from you. How has your week been?"

"Uneventful." She replied after a moment's pause. Other than her weird dreams, nothing else had happened. She had been very careful with the blood she took from the hospital, so she wouldn't need to *change*. Ever since Monday, when she'd felt herself dying, she worried about being anything other than human.

"That's good. I was just about to fix dinner. Are you hungry?" He asked, without thinking. They had never discussed whether she needed anything other than blood. He closed his eyes, almost dreading her answer.

The invitation both surprised and pleased Nada. He had actually invited her into his home. "Yes, I am, thank you."

Grady sighed, "Great. There are a few more questions I wanted to ask you. I hope you don't mind if I ask them over dinner?"

"No, of course not." She reached into her purse to write down his address below the number on the back of his business card. "I just got home from work, so give me an hour to shower and change."

"I'll see you then."

Nada arrived in just under an hour. The potatoes were baking, and Grady had just turned the steaks. He pulled the wine out of the fridge and headed for the door. He pulled it open and stepped back, smiling upon seeing Nada. She wore a light cotton mini dress with spaghetti straps. The pastel color complimented her milky skin. She had pulled up the sides of her long hair and fastened them with barrettes.

He was about to invite her in, when he remembered another vampire myth. They couldn't go into a person's home without being invited. He stepped away from the door and held an arm out, gesturing the living room. "Good evening."

Nada stepped forward, holding her hands toward him. As she stepped over the threshold, he finally noticed she held something.

"I didn't want to come empty handed. I don't bake, so I got this at the grocery store," she blushed lightly.

Grady looked at the pie she held and almost admitted he had just tested her. He was glad she had passed but doubted she'd appreciate the humor of the situation. "You didn't have to bring anything." He took it from her, "but I guess it's good you did. I didn't even think about dessert."

Nada smiled and nodded, before stepping past him to head for the living room. Two cats sat on the couch, and she froze upon seeing them. They reared up when they saw her, and both hissed. Nada covered her mouth, afraid that she would let out another hiss. Her mouth felt fuller, and her teeth felt longer. Running her tongue over them, a few even felt sharper. When Grady swore, her attention went back to him.

"Damn, I never even thought." He raced toward the cats, but they didn't need any prompting. They ran from the room, and he followed them, closing a door behind them. He turned back to Nada with an apologetic smile. "Sorry about that. Are you OK?"

She still covered her mouth and took a deep breath. Running her tongue over her teeth again, they felt normal. Had she just imagined them *changing*? The same thing happened when she felt threatened in one of her current dreams. The lines between fantasy and reality began to blur for her. How did she know she wasn't dreaming right then? "I'm fine," Nada replied, nodding. She lowered her hand and stepped forward, looking around the room. She decided she must be awake, since none of her dreams ever took place inside. "You have a lovely home. I'd ask for a tour, but I'm afraid we'd run into more animals." She finally smiled.

Grady chuckled and looked toward the back door. His greyhound stared through the glass, his eyes fixed on Nada. Grady placed the pie on the bar before walking over and closing the drapes. "Nah, there aren't any others inside, and the cats will stay in my room as long as you're here." He hadn't considered that animals would be able to sense that Nada wasn't like other humans. He tried not to think of it negatively. If he'd brought in a strange cat or any other animal, his cats would have reacted the same way. Pets never liked a foreign animal invading their territory. Grady looked at Nada in her pretty dress and found it hard to consider her a foreign animal.

Nada tried to smile but had to fight the disappointment at not being able to see his bedroom, even though she didn't know why that would be important. She looked down, hoping to hide the emotion in her gaze. Why did he have to have so many animals? Weren't the ones at his clinic enough?

"Am I right in assuming you can *morph* into any animal you feed on?" He asked quickly.

She nearly flinched at the unexpected question. "That is probably correct, though I doubt I'll ever attempt to *change* into a mouse."

The comment struck Grady as extremely funny, and he threw back his head to laugh. He couldn't get the image out of his head. Would she actually be able to shrink down that small or would she just be a huge mouse? A sobering thought abruptly halted his laughter.

"Have you ever fed on a human?"

Nada smiled at his laughter but almost jumped at the silence when it suddenly ceased. His unwanted question wasn't exactly unexpected, and she looked away.

"Nada?" Grady prodded. "Have you?" The timer went off just then, and Nada looked toward the kitchen.

"You did say we would talk over dinner," she reminded him.

Grady nodded and headed for the kitchen, but he didn't take his eyes off her. He remembered her reaction when he mentioned the bodies found drained of blood. "Have you ever killed a human, Nada?"

"No, Grady, I haven't," she answered honestly.

She answered that quickly, which brought him back to the question she hadn't answered, "but you have fed on them?"

Nada shifted, uncomfortable with the way he looked at her. She began to regret coming, and tears filled her eyes.

"Naturally, it's my blood of choice. Do you think I like turning into animals?" She replied, more than a little defensively.

Grady took a deep breath and sighed, as he started to load up their plates. "I'm sorry, Nada. It's just that your evasiveness scares me a bit."

"I have a feeling that's not the only thing about me that scares you. I've never directly fed from a human, Grady. I work around donated blood. That is where I get it from."

He carried the plates to the table and poured the wine. He drank about half the contents of his glass before refilling it. "Then why do you need to kill the animals?" He walked around the table and pulled out a chair for her. She slowly approached and sat down.

Nada watched him walk back into the kitchen and bring back the salad and the pie she brought. He avoided looking directly at her, as he moved about the two rooms. "Damn it, Grady, look at me!" She nearly yelled.

He spun around to stare at her. "What's wrong?"

"What's wrong?" She repeated. "I feel like I'm being interrogated. It hasn't been easy for me, you know?"

Grady finally noticed her eyes swam with tears. He watched her impatiently wipe them away before they could fall. "I can only imagine."

"That's right, and you are so lucky because of it. I've never told anyone about this, and now you know why. I can't even spend too much time with normal people, since I'm always afraid of something happening. I've never wanted them to treat me like you just did." She paused to take a slow deep breath. "I'll answer any question you have, but just so long as you understand you may not like all the answers."

She looked at the food in front of her. It smelled good, but she had lost her appetite. Of course, she would force herself to eat, since she wouldn't want to offend Grady. He had put a lot of work into their dinner. When she looked back up, he sat in the chair across from her.

"I'm sorry, Nada," he said softly.

She almost groaned at his compassionate look. Nada swallowed the lump in her throat and looked back at her food. "It looks wonderful. Thank you for dinner."

"You're welcome. Dig in." He picked up his knife and fork but waited for her to start. He watched as she cut off a piece of the steak and put it in her mouth. She chewed for a moment before looking at him with a small smile.

"It's delicious." She swallowed the food in her mouth and took a sip from her water glass, thankful that he had given her something to drink besides the wine. She hadn't told him that she didn't like to drink alcohol. She never drank wine and briefly wondered if it would have the same effect as liquor.

Grady watched every move she made. She regained her composure quickly, but he knew she was still upset. He didn't think she wanted to admit to him how hard her life had been.

"Don't you have any friends?" He finally asked.

"Just the people I work with, though I don't see them often," she replied without looking up.

He shook his head. "I'm the first person you've told this to?" The rhetorical question didn't need a response, but Nada nodded slowly. She finally looked up to meet his gaze.

"What do you do with your free time?" He asked as he realized what a lonely life she must lead.

She shrugged and took a deep breath. "I work double shifts most of the time. When I'm off, I keep busy." She finished evasively.

Grady wouldn't hear of it. "Doing what?" He pressed.

She sighed. "I like to run and work out. I draw what strikes my interest and sometimes I watch what's on TV. Mostly, I like to sleep."

"You sleep?" He repeated.

"Yeah, I like to dream." She paused for a moment. "At least I used to."

"What happened?"

Nada looked down at her steak, not yet ready to talk about that. She shook her head and picked up her knife and fork. "A pint of blood will usually last me two days. As long as everything is normal in my life, I can go quite a while without having to *change*. If I'm overly exhausted or careless, I run out before I can get more from work. Sometimes I wake up needing blood that I don't have in my apartment. My body doesn't give me much time before it takes over. I don't always get to decide when an animal will emerge. Once I have *changed*, I cannot become human again until I feed, and the animal needs much more blood than I do." She took a deep breath. Grady's mouth hung open, as if he wanted to speak but didn't know what to say. Nada smiled at him. She ate the entire time, and nearly finished half of her steak. Her appetite returned while she talked.

"I guess you don't want to talk about your dreams?" He commented, amazed how she could eat and talk at the same time without looking offensive. He watched her mouth the entire time and hadn't once seen food. Did she even chew?

She winced a bit. "Not yet."

"OK, so you've never attacked a human as an animal?" He asked doubtfully.

She shook her head while continuing to look at the plate in front of her. The red juice surrounding the rest of her steak mesmerized her. She tore off a piece of her roll and sopped up the liquid as if it were gravy. She popped it into her mouth and chewed slowly.

Grady watched her face closely, mesmerized by her changing expressions. He caught himself right before he licked his lips and mentally shook himself. Her pleasured expression didn't come from passion or his cooking, but from the cow's blood. Grady closed his eyes for a second and cleared his throat.

"How do you know?" Just as he asked it, Grady remembered how she had left his clinic as an owl but returned as a human. Nada's gaze slowly lifted to meet his. He briefly wondered if she could read his mind, or if she had sharp enough ears to hear his breath catch. "You have memories of when you're an animal?"

"It didn't start out that way," she said with a nod, "but now I am conscious of what is going on *while* I'm in animal form."

His expression grew distasteful. "So you're aware of killing animals while you're doing it? How can you stomach it?"

She leaned back in her seat and sighed, trying to think of a good way of putting it. The disgust in his voice rubbed her the wrong way, but she tried to ignore it. After all, how would she feel if their situations were reversed? Would she have helped him at all? Nada looked up and finally noticed the vaulted ceiling. When she realized she was about to comment on how it accentuated the room, she looked back at Grady. Her eyes narrowed slightly to still see distaste curling the edges of his mouth.

"It's sort of like an out of body experience. I witness everything that is going on, but the animal instinct has primary control. Anything that is normal to whatever animal I am at that time seems normal enough to me while it's happening. Besides, by that time I'm in such dire need of blood, nothing else matters."

Grady put his utensils down and took another swallow of his wine. "If that's true, then can you honestly say you wouldn't attack a human if the need were that great?"

She blinked a few times as she thought about what he said. It reminded her of the full moon, but she had seen enough fear in his eyes already. She didn't want to experience the terror that admission would ensue. "My morals won't allow me to take a human life. Those morals seem to stay with me when I *change*." She took a swallow of wine. Its warmth flowed through her, almost like blood did, and she smiled. "I've not killed a human yet in all the time I've been like this. I think those are pretty good odds."

"How old are you, Nada?"

"Twenty-nine," she responded.

He nodded, disappointed. "So you won't know for a while whether or not you'll have an extended life." If she said fifty, at least he'd know her condition made her appear younger, although he wouldn't have guessed her to be in her late twenties. "So you were normal up until you were around twenty-seven? What were you doing when it happened?"

She shrugged. "I was in Europe at that time. Nothing is clear until I woke up one morning in Germany. I don't even know for sure that's where it happened, but my blood thirst started right after I got back to the states."

"And you have no idea what changed you?" He hated to think of her being dishonest, but could her amnesia be real? Or was the event so traumatic, her mind wouldn't allow her to remember it? That seemed likely, if some creature attacked her and joined with her somehow. He tried to think of the possibilities of how an uncharted DNA could merge with her own human DNA, not to mention the varied animal DNA that followed. He was out of his depth and wondered what to do next.

Nada shook her head but didn't speak. He gave her a moment to respond, but her mouth remained closed. He suddenly wished he knew how to hypnotize. It was all locked in that pretty head of hers, but what would those memories do to her once she remembered? He realized she needed a shrink and regretted that he wasn't one.

Neither of them was too talkative after that. He cut them each a piece of the pie she brought, but hers remained untouched. Grady finally told her he'd think about it for a while and then get back with her. Nada seemed relieved by the apparent dismissal and left quickly. He still sat at the table a few hours later, wondering what to do next.

As if in answer, the phone rang. The cordless lay beside him, and he reached for it.

"Dr. Duncan?"

"That's how you answer your home phone?" Grady heard Kiefer chuckle. "Do you think I'd impress the chicks by answering 'Dr. Taylor'?"

Grady smiled. "You don't need help in that department, pal. What's up?" He shook his head. Kiefer knew he didn't answer his home phone with such a formal greeting. He'd just been distracted, but Kiefer's next question got his full attention.

"I just wanted to let you know I'm going out of town for a few days. Do you have a problem looking out for the place?"

"No, of course not." Grady already planned his phone call to Nada. "Do you mind if a friend and I use the weight room?"

"Oooh, got a girlfriend already? You still got the keys, right?"

Grady rolled his eyes. "They're around here some-where." A chuckle on the other end followed his response.

"Just checking. Let me know if you ever need me to look after your animals."

"I'll hold you to that, Kiefer. By the way, no, I don't have a girlfriend."

"Sure thing, pal. See you when I get back."

After Grady hung up, he looked at the clock.

# Chapter Seven

When Nada got home, she didn't feel as good as she had after her first meeting with Grady. She feared he knew too much about her. The amnesia seemed to trouble him the most, but she couldn't do anything about that. She had never felt more helpless. She knew it also bothered him that she killed animals for their blood. For the first time she wondered if she could control herself enough to take just what she needed and leave the animal alive. She never tried that before and didn't know if she could do it. She knew that she could subsist on a cup of human blood a day, so there shouldn't be any reason why she couldn't do the same after she *changed*. For Grady's sake she would at least try. She ignored the voice that reminded her of the full moon. She would deal with that when she had to in three weeks. Nada didn't always kill during the full moon, which puzzled her. There had been plenty of times she had awoken with the worst thirst of her life. She had even awoken just to *change* again, so her body could immediately get what it needed. It seemed the only time she could turn back into a human without feeding was during the full moon. She wondered many times what she did during that one night a month.

Nada dropped her purse and keys on the couch and collapsed next to them. She didn't even want to turn on the television. She rested her head on a pillow and closed her eyes. The next thing she knew, the phone rang.

As she reached for the extension, she glanced at the clock. She had been asleep for two hours. "Hello?"

"I didn't wake you, did I?" Grady asked.

Nada smiled and leaned back into the cushions. Grady convinced her to give him her phone number before leaving his home. She also relented and told him her last name. She figured she had trusted him with so much already, that there really was no need not to trust him completely. She didn't expect him to call so soon, but it pleased her to hear his voice. She loved his soothing tones, even when he felt stressed. "Not really. I was just resting on the couch."

"That's good. Do you have any free time this weekend or next week?" He asked.

"Whenever I'm not working is free time." She replied, stifling a yawn. "What's up?"

"I couldn't stop thinking about you after you left here. I've been replaying in my head every conversation and meeting we've had. I've noticed a few things about you that I'd like to test."

"Test? What have you noticed?" *Besides the obvious*, she finished silently.

"Your reflexes for one thing. You're graceful and quick, and I wonder if it's normal for you, or if it's a *morphing* side effect."

Nada sat up. "How would you test that?"

"There's a physical therapy clinic next door to my clinic. Doctor Taylor and I look after each other's offices at times, so I have a key. He's got a treadmill and weights. What do you think?" Grady asked, holding his breath.

Nada stared at the black screen of her television and blinked a few times. She couldn't see anything wrong with the unusual request. "Sure," she replied and smiled. "As long as it doesn't interfere with watching my man, I'm up for it."

There was a pause. "I thought you said you didn't have any friends?"

The smile started first before Nada began to laugh. Her infectious laugh stunned Grady, since he hadn't heard it before. Being too surprised to join in, he decided he would have to make sure she had a lot to laugh about, no matter what it took. "What's so funny?" He finally asked.

Her laughter ended quickly, and soon she just smiled again. "Nothing...it's just a TV show I watch, about a good vampire that defeats evil ones. I was being silly."

Grady nodded, forgetting she couldn't see him. "You actually watch shows like that?"

"Never miss an episode. I don't watch much television, but I guess I sort of relate to the good guy. Strange, huh?" Knowing she didn't want to go into detail on the subject, she fell silent. Especially since her favorite vampire's poster still lay crumpled in her trash.

"Not so strange, Nada. I think it would be harder for you to relate to something that was evil."

"You don't think I'm evil, then?" She asked.

"No, of course not." He quickly responded.

She smiled and felt warm all over. She had been afraid to ask him what he thought of her. He was a veterinarian and loved animals, and she had killed plenty of them.

Since Nada had to work too many hours over the weekend, she couldn't meet with Grady until Monday. She arrived at his clinic a few minutes after it closed. She tried the door to find it unlocked, so she walked in.

"Grady?" She called out.

"I'll be right there." His voice came from his office.

She clutched her keys and waited. She felt a little nervous to be tested and wondered what the findings would reveal. Never having stepped foot in a gym, she didn't even know the level of her own strength.

Grady left his office and looked toward the front door. When his gaze fell on Nada, he almost stumbled. He previously saw her naked but had been too shocked to notice much about her body. He smiled as he took in her appearance. Her long hair tapered up into a ponytail, and she wore a pink sports bra with white shorts. The thigh length shorts showed off her thin but muscular legs. Ordinarily, such pale skin would look sickly, but her skin nearly glowed. As she adjusted her hair, the muscles in her arms flexed. Grady looked down her body to see her outfit finished off with pink socks and sneakers.

"Will this do?"

His gaze rose to her face when she spoke. He nodded slowly, wanting to walk over and caress one of her milky smooth arms. She truly captivated him.

Following him to the next office, she waited for him to unlock the door. He stepped aside so that she could enter first. He then reached over and turned on the light switch. "It's through that door." He pointed to the second door on the left.

Nada walked forward and opened the door. She stepped into the room and placed her keys on a wall hook. Looking from the treadmill in the corner to the free weights, her gaze rested on the weight machine in the center of the room. Several different areas of the body could be worked on by using different sides of the machine, but all used the single stack of weights in the center.

Grady walked in behind her. "We'll start with the treadmill, but I need to get your vitals first." He directed her to the scale.

Nada raised her eyebrows, not having weighed in years. She stepped onto the scale, while Grady slid the weights around.

"102," he finally said and wrote the number on a chart.   He then measured her height at 5'1" and wrote that down.   He pulled out a tape measure and wrote down her bust, waist and hip measurements. He then calculated her body fat at 12%, which was very low for a woman. Grady told her to have a seat, so he could test her vitals. She had normal blood pressure, but her temperature registered a high 99.8 degrees.   Nada nodded.

"It always runs a bit high."

"Alright, then I guess that's it." It was on the tip of his tongue to comment on the fact that most animals' body temperatures ranged higher than humans, but he didn't think she'd care to hear that. "You can get on the treadmill now."

He started her walking, not knowing if she needed a good warm up first. After two minutes, he increased the speed until she jogged. He then continued to increase the speed until she ran. "If you feel it's going too fast, let me know."

She nodded, and he continued to raise the speed. He watched her legs as she ran. It amazed him that her feet didn't make more noise when they struck the tread, but he couldn't hear anything above the machine's engine. Her run still looked comfortable, so he raised the speed again. Wondering at her speed, he looked at the readout. He gasped to see 38 MPH on the readout. He swung his head around to look at her, surprised to see her breathing unlabored. Shaking his head, he increased the speed again.  Grady walked around the treadmill so that he could see her from every angle. Her skin began to glisten with a fine layer of perspiration. The movement of muscle beneath damp skin so absorbed him that he nearly forgot to check the readout. By the time the machine reached 60, he could barely see her legs moving. Nada moved her body forward at the hips, and he half expected her to start running on all fours. His mouth fell open as he raised the speed in one-mile increments. His fingers moved to raise it more, when he heard her voice.

"Grady," she rasped. He looked at her face, and she shook her head. He hit the emergency stop button.

Nada grabbed the sides of the machine and gasped for air.  Her cheeks were bright red, and sweat broke out on her face. "Damn, that nearly killed me."

Grady handed her some water, and she gulped it down. "How fast was I going?" She finally asked. He wrote on her chart and noted the time. Nada looked at the clock across the room and noticed a half-hour had passed. No wonder she was tired.

"You were going 67 when I stopped it." He thought about the few other animals that could run that fast. He wondered if she remembered feeding on a cheetah but couldn't bring himself to ask. He grabbed a towel from the shelf and handed it to her.

"67 miles per hour?" She asked, finding it hard to believe. She knew she could run fast, but she never pushed herself that hard before.  She wiped the towel across her damp face.

"Yeah. I wouldn't have believed it had I not seen for myself.  I can't wait to see how strong you are."

"Me, too." She agreed.

Grady ran her through all four sides of the weight bench. Her arms could bench up to 200 pounds, and her legs could do over 500. He gave up on counting how many ab-crunches she could do, as well as pushups.

"Where do you get all this energy?" He finally asked her. Merely watching her made him tired.

She stopped half way through a pushup and looked at him. She fed earlier in the day and suddenly realized she hadn't anticipated working out to such an extreme. Pushing up to her knees, she realized her body would need more blood. Her hair pulled free from her ponytail, and she flung it over her shoulder. The extra motion made her a little light headed, and she sat back on her heels.

"Grady?" She started but faltered. She hadn't been paying attention but now noticed the slight headache. She couldn't get any more blood until the next day at work. Her hand moved up to cover her mouth.

"What's wrong, Nada?" He knelt in front of her and placed his hands on her knees.

She looked at his hands. Her knees grew hot beneath his warm skin. Her gaze moved up to his eyes, as she became aware of feeling the blood flowing through his hands. She could then pick up his heartbeat. Standing abruptly, she pushed Grady away. He caught his balance at the last minute.

"Stay away," she cautioned, holding up a hand. She looked around the room, feeling like a caged animal.

"Nada?"

She barely heard his voice, but she didn't want to *change* in front of him again. She fled the room, pulling her clothes off as she went. Grady only saw a blur, but he attempted to follow. He found her shorts by the front door, and he ran outside. Her socks and shoes were together a few feet away, but she was nowhere to be seen. He looked up and saw a large bird flying out of sight. "Damn!" He yelled as he leaned down to retrieve her shorts, socks and shoes.

Grady ran back inside and grabbed her keys from the hook, and her bra from the floor. He locked up the clinic and ran out to Nada's car. He held the keys in his hand a moment before unlocking the driver's side door. He found her wallet in the glove box and searched for her license. He looked at the picture first and noticed the radiant smile and the tan skin. He looked closer at Nada's picture. She *was* tan, but then he noticed the issue date. The license was over three years old, so the Nada he looked at was completely human.

Her birth date was next to the issue date. She would be turning 30 on October 13th, less than three weeks away. He smiled, as he looked at her name, relieved she hadn't lied to him. He read the address below and cringed. It listed an address out of state. He rummaged through the wallet until he found her insurance card, which listed a local address. He started her car and drove it to that address.

Grady let himself into Nada's apartment. He put her keys, wallet and clothing on the coffee table. He looked around the combination living room and dining room. A bar separated it from the kitchen. The only other door stood open. He walked over to it and looked into her bedroom. Not wanting to invade her privacy more than he already had, he didn't go in. He walked back to the kitchen and got himself a glass of water, half tempted to open the fridge.

Resisting the urge, he walked back to the couch, and the easel caught his eye. Nada mentioned drawing but he had been too distracted to ask about it. Grady walked closer and stared in awe. When she completed the sketch, it should be displayed in a museum. He reached forward to touch but stopped just shy of it. Since it was pencil, he didn't want to smudge it. Grady looked out the window and realized the scene must have come from her memory. That fact alone made her talent more impressive. He couldn't take his eyes from the sketch for several moments, before looking around the room for more. When he didn't see any, he wondered if she stored them. Maybe she kept them in her room, but he didn't want to snoop. Looking back at the easel, he noticed the drawing was on a large sketchpad. Picking it up, he flipped to the first page and gasped. The beach scene took him by surprise. He couldn't even picture Nada's pale skin being exposed to the sun. He glanced at the bottom and noticed the date. She drew it six months earlier. Remembering the tan face in her driver's license, Grady surmised that before Europe, Nada had been more active. She might even have had a boyfriend. He flipped through the rest of the pictures, but stopped on a couple embracing. The detail of their kiss was exceptional. Every line and curve and shadow was perfect. Grady swallowed hard as he flipped to the last unfinished drawing and replaced the pad on the easel. He walked back to the couch and sat down. As he looked around her home, he wondered if he should drive back to the clinic and wait for her there? Something told him she wouldn't go back there, but he felt like such an intruder. As Grady wondered how long he would be waiting, he turned on the television.

A little less than an hour later, he heard the flapping of wings as a hawk flew into the room. When she saw Grady, she let out a squawk and flew into the bedroom. Tempted to follow, he didn't, even through the lengthy wait. He heard a muffled curse and then water running. A half-hour later, Nada walked back into the living room wearing a robe.

"How...what are you doing here?" She asked in a shaky voice, running her fingers through her freshly washed hair. She had been quite shocked to fly in and see him sitting on her couch and almost waited on her shower. Deciding she would rather be clean, she made him wait.

He held up her key ring. She looked at it for a moment before looking back at him.

"How did you know I wouldn't go back to the clinic?" She asked accusingly. "I would have needed my things."

"Call it a hunch, Nada. I didn't think you would expect me to wait there, let alone expect your clothes to be where you left them. I thought you would prefer to have your car and things brought to your home."

"Yes, it's my home. This is my one safe place, and you've invaded it." She didn't know which emotion was stronger, the need to cry or to yell. Her eyes focused on her stack of clothes and shoes on the coffee table. If not for him, she would have had to take a taxi to her car. Someone probably would have stolen her shoes. She ceased her pacing and calmed down as she realized he was only trying to help. "So my car is here, too?" She asked quietly.

Grady nodded. "Why don't you sit down and relax? I thought you might want to talk about what happened."

She sat on the edge of the couch and stared across the room. "I should have known better. A cup of blood isn't enough if I overexert myself."

Grady nodded, again. "If I ask you something, will you be honest with me?"

She looked at him and hesitantly nodded.

"You've told me that you've never fed directly from a human, and I do believe you. The thing I'm wondering is whether you *want* to feed from a human?"

Nada had the strongest desire to start chewing her nails. "Why do you ask that?"

"Why did you push me away at the clinic?" He countered.

She bit her lip in consternation and took a deep breath. "It's not as if I *want* to feed from a human, Grady. It's more like I *need* to. Most of the time I'm fine, though. It's just when I need blood and a human gets too close to me. You got too close." She hated to admit that, since she wanted him to get close to her. "I mean physically too close at the wrong time. I really don't think I could ever hurt you, but I don't want to find out otherwise. I'm sorry I pushed you, but I had to get away. You've seen what I'm capable of when I'm an animal. It scares me to think I can do that kind of damage when I'm human. I even tried not to kill the animal I fed on earlier, but I wasn't able to control it."

She shocked Grady speechless for a moment. He knew her strength, thanks to the tests he performed, but now he realized how much that strength exceeded his. "That's why you don't like to be around people?"

"One of the reasons, yes."

"It's good that you tried to control yourself. What kind of animal was it this time?"

She shrugged, "A gopher."

"Can you *morph* into humans that you've fed from?" He asked suddenly.

At first she didn't understand the question, but it slowly occurred to her. "You mean the actual person?"

He nodded. "I mean if you fed from me, could you *morph* to look like me?"

As bad as she had been feeling, his question actually lifted her spirits. She couldn't do something that worried him about her. "No, Grady, when I feed, I can only turn into the species, not the individual. To be more specific than that, I can only *change* into a female of that species, even if I fed on a male. Since I'm already human, feeding on a human wouldn't make any difference."

"So you tried it and it didn't work, huh?" He sighed, almost ashamed of the relief he felt.

She frowned at the question. "I guess you could say that."

The frown puzzled him. "What is it?"

She thought about her answer before speaking. She couldn't imagine changing into something that wasn't primitive. She always had to picture in her mind what she wanted to change into. Her own face was the only human face she had ever pictured. She had no idea what any of the people who donated blood looked like. The chill that ran down her spine troubled her. "Nothing really. It would probably be nice to be able to change into other people instead of always animals." She ended with a half smile.

Grady almost shook his head. "You really have no memory of your life before all this started?"

She had been staring across the room, but his question brought her gaze back to him. Nada looked into his hazel eyes for a moment and slowly shook her head. "I don't even remember what my parents looked like. All

I know is that I lost them when I was young. I don't remember going to college, but I have the degree. Nothing is clear until I was twenty-seven in Germany. I don't know how I got there, but luckily I found my passport and was able to come back to the U.S." She looked inquisitive for a moment. "Do you think I'm lying to you about not remembering what happened to me?" She met his stare without blinking, and he looked away first. He shook his head but didn't respond. When he remained silent, she continued. "I may not volunteer everything, but I'll never lie to you. I can't afford to lose the only friend I have, can I?"

"Do you have friends when you dream?" He asked, putting her honesty to the test. He noticed her flinch, since she obviously did not want to talk about that yet.

Nada looked toward her bedroom and swallowed hard. She still stared at it when she answered. "Not anymore."

Grady reached out and touched her hand. Her gaze met his again. "Nada, what's wrong?"

She shrugged her slim shoulders then drew her knees up to her chest. The hem of the robe hugged her ankles as she wrapped her arms around her legs. "Awhile ago I discovered that I could pretty much control what I dream about. At first I tried to be normal in my dreams, but I don't know what that is. Nothing felt right, no matter where I went or what I did. Finally, I didn't change who I was but instead took people with me that I had more in common with." She paused to suddenly smile.

Her smile mesmerized Grady, as it made her look so peaceful. It was the first time he had seen that expression on her lovely features. Not wanting her to stop talking, he kept his mouth shut and waited for Nada to continue.

"Once I started doing that, I looked forward to going to sleep at night. It changed my life." She focused on Grady and studied his face. "I don't know what I would have done had I not discovered those dreams. The idea that no one could ever love me the way I am, well, it's hard to bear sometimes. I'm loved in my dreams...Well, at least I was."

"What's different now?"

She shook her head. "I don't know, but they're ending badly." She got choked up just thinking about what she was about to say. "I don't know if I can trust them enough to go into them again, but how can I go back to not having them?" She stood and walked across the room. She wiped her eyes as Grady stared at her back. As hard as her life had been the last few years, she never cried about it. It was strange how easily the tears came since she met Grady.

To break the uncomfortable silence, Grady pointed at the sketchpad. "How long have you been sketching? Those are really great."

Nada smiled as she turned around. She wiped away the tears from her flushed face, appreciating the subject change. If he stood closer to her, she might have been tempted to hug him. As she thought about the question, she chuckled softly. "I don't know, but thanks. Sometimes, I draw the places I'd like to escape to in my dreams."

"They really are exceptional, Nada."

She gazed across the room at her current unfinished sketch, but his words drew her eyes back to him. Instead of speaking, she bit her lower lip and nodded.

Grady returned the nod, before standing and clearing his throat. "Well, I guess I've taken up enough of your time. Let me know if you want to work on not killing those animals. I'll be happy to help you, if I can."

"I'm open to any suggestions."

Grady shrugged and felt a little foolish. Should he even have made the offer? What could he do? Wasn't it more important to find out what happened to make her different? As he stared at the hopeful look on her face, he took a deep breath. He wasn't a psychiatrist. Until her memory came back, he could nothing about that. He was trained to work with animals, and he was all she had. He knew he would sleep better knowing that no more animals would die. He had the feeling it would give her a measure of peace, too. "Let me think about it for a few days. I'll come up with something."

She nodded and walked him to the door. He paused in front of it and turned. "I hope you do know that you're safe with me and can tell me anything. As long as I'm confident you're not a threat, I wouldn't turn you in. If you're honest with me, there's no reason for me to doubt that."

She smiled and reached an arm toward him. She placed her hand on his shoulder and pulled him toward her. He almost resisted but leaned closer. Thinking she wanted to whisper something in his ear, she surprised him by lightly kissing him on the cheek.

"Thank you, Grady. I'm glad I met you, and I'll try not to disappoint you or abuse your trust in me." She bit her, and blinked her watery eyes.

He straightened then nodded in response. "I know that, Nada." He gave her shoulder a quick comforting squeeze, then turned and left.

# Chapter Eight

Except for a few phone conversations, Nada didn't see Grady the rest of the week. She found herself missing him, so she worked extra hours at the hospital to keep her mind occupied. Saturday would be her next day off, and she already told Grady that it was her turn to fix him dinner. Afterwards, he wanted them to start working on getting her used to not killing the animals she fed from. She wondered how he would help her with that problem.

She got home from work the night before their date, or appointment, whichever was more accurate. She'd like to think of it as a date but had enough sense to know that Grady saw her as one of his patients. In his eyes she was just another animal. Since he loved animals, she guessed that wasn't so bad.

Nada made a grocery list of items she would need for their meal on Saturday. As she stuck the list on the fridge with a magnet, she noticed the calendar next to it. Saturday was the last day of September, so she went ahead and tore off the old month. After she did that, her gaze went to the second week of October. *Full moon* was printed in the box for the second Friday of the month. She only had two weeks to go, and she cringed.

Nada stared at the mountains in the dark, wondering why they seemed so familiar. She had no trouble seeing anything, since she could see much better at night than during the day. That probably explained why she didn't like being out in sunlight. Her eyes were too sensitive to its brightness. A cloud moved away from the moon, and she noticed its fullness. It didn't even cross her mind that she still had two weeks until the next full moon. It seemed perfectly natural for her to be staring at it.

She looked back at the mountains, ignoring the fact she didn't live near any. The cool air caressed her, but she didn't feel chilled. She looked down at her arms, only to discover black paws. She stared at them without surprise, since she always *changed* during a full moon. Being conscious during it did surprise her though. She didn't recognize the animal she changed into, so she headed for the nearby lake. She stared at her reflection to see a panther staring back. A low growl caught her attention, and she turned quickly.

Another black panther approached from the woods. She moved away from the lake and slowly walked toward him. As she stared at him, he pushed up onto his hind legs. He continued walking, and his legs changed from animal to human. Her gaze dropped to his crotch, which also *changed* into a man's dick. His transformation awed her so much that she didn't notice her own body doing the same thing. Black hair still covered them, but the lower halves of their bodies turned human. Their paws turned into hands, then fingers grew where there had been claws, and then Nada noticed her breasts beginning to form. She waited for the rest of the *change* to happen, but it didn't. Both of them kept their panther heads, backs and tails. Since she had never been able to partially *change* from one species to the next, she hadn't thought it possible.

By then the male reached her. He circled her, running his hand possessively across her breasts and then her back. She couldn't tell if she knew him and didn't know why she didn't run from him. His touch nearly hypnotized her. As he continued to caress her, she finally noticed his erection. Her mouth fell open, but she didn't speak or object.

When he took her hand, she followed. He led her to a boulder and pushed her onto it. She reached out to keep from falling on it and felt him rubbing against her backside. He reached around with both hands and fondled her breasts. She felt her legs being forced apart, as he pushed her face into the boulder. She placed her hands under her face to protect it from the rock's surface. Luckily, the boulder was relatively smooth, since her stomach and the front of her thighs smashed into it when he impaled her from behind. She gasped as he filled her completely.

As he rode her, it troubled Nada to realize she enjoyed it. Since she couldn't remember much of her past, she couldn't recall ever having sex before. As the pleasure began to build, she arched into the male. He must have been pretty close to his climax, too, as he moved a hand to her left shoulder. His fingers dug into her throat as he matched her movements to his. She dropped her head against him, but then he opened his jaw. She saw the glint of his sharp teeth, right before he sank them into her right shoulder.

Nada awoke screaming. She tried to get out of bed but got tangled in the sheets and fell off the side. Her chin hit the floor hard, but that didn't stop her. She rolled over and attempted to jump up but got caught up in the sheet. She landed on her butt and kicked out her feet. As she vaulted away from the bed, she ripped the sheet in her attempt to be free of it, and her back slammed into the wall. She slid down to the floor, and her gaze flew about the room. When she saw no one else, she took deep breaths in an attempt to calm down. She never had a nightmare like that before and hoped it never happened again.

Nada stood and backed out of the room. When she reached the bathroom, she turned to the mirror and looked at her shoulder in the reflection. She half expected to see teeth marks, but there was nothing. She looked at her chin, to see blood running down her neck. She then remembered falling out of bed and winced. Grabbing a washcloth, she pressed it against her chin. "Damn!" She muttered, and she thought her dreams with her favorite vampire had been bad. She'd take those any day over what had just happened. She jumped when someone started knocking on her door.

"Nada! Are you all right? Nada!" The pounding got worse, and Nada walked through her room to the living room. She pulled open the door to see her neighbor standing there. The old woman looked scared to death.

"Honey, are you OK? That scream was blood curdling."

Nada stared at the fragile woman and tried not to smile. Nothing about the situation was funny, but her neighbor obviously didn't take the time to get dressed. She stood in her doorway wearing nothing but a threadbare robe barely tied about the waist. "Yes, Mrs. Jenkins, I'm fine. I just had a nightmare and fell out of bed."

"Are you sure? That sure is a lot of blood." Mrs. Jenkins replied, pointing at the bloody washcloth.

Nada pulled the cloth away from her face, surprised at the amount of blood. "Yes, I'm fine, but I need to take care of this. Thank you for your concern, Mrs. Jenkins. I'm sorry I woke you. Goodnight." She closed the door before the woman could say anything else. Nada leaned against the door, and her whole body shook. She pressed harder on the cloth against her chin. If she *changed*, then the wound would be healed by the time she became human again, but she would have to feed. Maybe if she chose a meek animal, she wouldn't need to kill. Nada looked at the fridge and got an idea. She ran over and pulled out the container of blood. She poured some of it into a bowl and heated it up. When it was warm, she placed the bowl on the floor and then made sure all her windows were locked. With that done, she pulled off her nightshirt and sat on the floor. She looked at the bowl and pictured a cat.

A few minutes later, a brown cat started walking around the apartment. Nada's initial instinct was to get outside so she could feed, but she attempted to take control of the animal. She let out a meow and paced in front of the window. One paw grazed the glass, before she could finally focus on the bowl in the kitchen. She licked her lips and jumped off the windowsill. Nada didn't realize how hard it would be to make the cat go against what it wanted to do, but her will eventually won.

She stopped at the bowl and sniffed the contents. Nada concentrated on the blood, convincing herself that she needed it. She slowly started lapping up the precious liquid. As it spread throughout her body, the lapping quickened. Before she knew it, the bowl was empty. She sat back and yowled, before curling up in a ball. Nada fought falling asleep, and instead concentrated on her human form.

Once she was again human, Nada stood and clapped her hands together. "Yes!" She declared triumphantly. It was possible to feed without killing. It hadn't been easy, and she doubted she could do it with a more aggressive animal, but she did it. She touched her chin and smiled, walking back into the bathroom to see her flawless chin. "Not even a scar." She couldn't wait to tell Grady.

Nada walked back into the living room to retrieve her nightshirt and the bloody washcloth. She threw them into the kitchen sink and picked up the bowl. She rinsed it out before placing it in the dishwasher. She then rinsed the washcloth and nightshirt before letting them soak in the sink with bleach water.

Nada turned to look at the clock. It was 4:00 in the morning. Poor Mrs. Jenkins. Luckily her scream hadn't given the old woman a heart attack. That reminded her of the nightmare. She had temporarily been able to forget about it, but it invaded her mind once again. She hoped it meant nothing, but it felt too real. She bit her lip as she debated telling Grady about it. Realizing she wanted his opinion, Nada decided to tell him.

She took a deep breath and knew it wouldn't be easy to get back to sleep. Too much had happened, and she anxiously wanted to talk to Grady. Though tempted to call him, she decided not to wake him. She'd see him soon enough. A hot bath sounded good. Maybe that would calm her down enough so that she could go back to bed. She nodded and headed to her bathroom.

# Chapter Nine

Nada hugged her pillow and stared at the shadows in her room. She tossed and turned for the last few hours, unable to get the nightmare out of her head. She had been unafraid of the male panther, even when she saw him *change*. She didn't want to think about the rest of the dream and instead concentrated on the male himself. She couldn't remember ever meeting another of her kind. That thought troubled her, and the image of a man with short black hair flashed across her mind. She couldn't picture his face, but she got chills thinking about him. Who was he, and why hadn't she ever thought about him before? Had it been the dream? Was he the panther? So many questions but no answers went through her thoughts. Would she dream about him again? Her final question to herself was whether or not she wanted to.

Nada groaned and got up. She started to make the bed, when she remembered ripping the sheet. She pulled it off the bed and tossed it into the trash. Pulling a new sheet out of the closet, she made the bed. She rubbed her flawless chin and shook her head. She had learned much about herself since Grady came into her life, and she looked forward to seeing him. She wanted to know what he would think of her nightmare. Changing into the cat and feeding without killing also excited her. She anxiously awaited knowing how he would help her work at feeding on animals without killing them.

Nada went shopping after she ate her breakfast. She wanted to get a new outfit along with the food she needed to prepare. She hadn't shopped for clothes in years so needed the salesgirl's help, who must've still been in high school. She convinced Nada that she *had* to get a black leather skirt. Nada already liked the color, but she didn't know how to feel about the snugness of the leather. In the end she bought it since she did agree that she looked great in it.

Nada didn't need any help choosing the lilac camisole. The silky material felt great on her skin. She looked at her reflection once she wore the entire ensemble and smiled. Leather and lace did work well together, she noted. As she continued her perusal in the mirror, the salesgirl spoke up.

"You know what would make that even better? Tan skin. There's this great tanning salon a few stores down. Their rates are really good."

Nada's gaze caught hers in the reflection and then looked back at her pale skin. She always avoided the sun, since it bothered her eyes. She was also more of a night person and was too active to lie still to get a tan.

The girl misunderstood her silence. "Not that you don't look good the way you are or anything. I've just always been partial to tans...what you do need though is spike heels. Would bring out those calf muscles. You must work out."

Nada cringed at the thought of high heels but a smile crept through. She couldn't imagine wearing anything she couldn't run in if needed. She opted for the flat ankle boots instead and surveyed her reflection again. She nodded with satisfaction.

The smile left her face when she wondered why she dressed to impress Grady. Was she hoping the outfit would get his attention? What good would that do when she already knew they didn't stand a chance? She shrugged it off; convincing herself the outfit was as much for her benefit as his. There couldn't be anything wrong with looking good.

When Nada got home, she put her new outfit on her bed and went back to the kitchen. She set out everything for their meal and pulled out the cookbook. After flipping to the recipe for Chicken Parmesan, she rinsed the meat. Grady phoned halfway through the preparation, wanting to check in to verify what time she expected him.

"Dinner will be ready by 6:00, but you can come early if you like."

"Sounds good. I have a few errands, but I should be there by 5:30."

Nada hung up and went back to the stove. She rubbed her temple and winced. Shaking her head, she walked over to the fridge to pull out the container of blood. She had hoped to postpone it as long as possible, since she wanted to be able to enjoy Grady being there without losing control. Once she poured herself a cup of the blood, she hid the container on the bottom shelf behind the butter. She didn't know if Grady would go into the fridge for some reason and wouldn't feel comfortable with him seeing the blood. She knew she was being silly, since he knew her secret, but that didn't change how she felt. It would be nice if they could have a normal dinner, without anything unusual coming up. She crossed her fingers while she waited for the blood to warm.

Grady arrived a little after 5:30. She smiled at his expression when she pulled open the door, relieved that she bought the new outfit. His eyes lit up when he saw her.

"Wow! You look great."

"Thanks." Her cheeks heated slightly. "Come in." She headed back to the kitchen, and Grady closed the door behind him. He followed her and put a bottle of wine on the counter.

"I never come empty handed, either. You seemed to like this when you were in my home."

Nada looked at the bottle and nodded. "It will go great with our dinner." He helped her set the table, and she served the salad. During their idle dinner conversation, Nada worked up the nerve to tell him about her dream. They had finished eating, when she decided to tell him. She asked him to have a seat on the couch, while she cleaned up the kitchen. He offered to help after complimenting her on the wonderful meal. Smiling her thanks, she insisted on her guest relaxing. She mainly wanted something to do so she could talk to him without having to look at him.

Once Nada finished telling Grady about her dream, he could only sit there and stare for a few moments. He took a sip of his wine and licked his suddenly dry lips. He cleared his throat and tried to swallow the lump that settled there. He took another sip of wine.

"That brings up a good point, though." He finally commented.

Nada dried her hands on the dishtowel and joined him on the couch. "What point?" She took a small sip of her wine.

"Have you ever tried to partially change into an animal?"

She shook her head. "I don't think it's possible."

"You've never tried then?" He prodded.

She shook her head, again. "That would take a lot more control than I have right now." She remembered their earlier conversation about her *morphing* into other humans. Could that be just another case of needing more control? She instinctively knew she couldn't *morph* into any male, but what about another woman? She couldn't see the need to and truly didn't think it even possible. Nada shoved it to the back of her mind.

She could see that her response puzzled him, so she continued. "It would be impossible to describe exactly what goes on in my head during a *change*." She paused as she searched for the words. "The closest I can come is to say that all animals have instincts. I don't think humans are too aware of them, since we have cars and homes and guns and so many other conveniences. Strip all that away, and you have just about every other mammal that is forced to live in nature."

Nada stopped and chewed on her lower lip. She didn't want to lose Grady by going off on a tangent, and the expression on his face revealed nothing. She sighed, focused her thoughts and continued. "The species of animal that I turn into brings its own instincts with it as I *change*. At least recently, I've been able to be aware, but it is difficult if not impossible to hold onto my human instincts. Can you follow that?" She asked, mentally crossing her fingers. She hadn't yet told him about being a cat earlier.

Grady slowly nodded. "You just said that only recently you've been aware while you're an animal. I would take that to mean that the longer you are this way, the more adapted to it you will become. Wouldn't you agree?"

"That follows." Nada replied with a reluctant nod.

"So it also follows that one day soon, you'll be able to partially change." He concluded.

"It was only a dream, Grady." She reminded him.

"Only a dream," he repeated. "It was that dream that triggered a memory of a man with dark hair, wasn't it? We don't live near any mountain lakes, Nada. Did they seem familiar to you? Were they in Europe? Which country? Was this man with you there?"

She shrugged. "It might be Germany, but I'm not sure. I can't remember all the countries I went to, and the man is only the faintest of memories. I can't picture his face or his name. Hell, he may not even exist."

"But you weren't afraid of him. You said so yourself. This half man/half panther forced himself on you, but you weren't afraid. At least not until he sunk his teeth into you."

Nada could tell that her dream bothered Grady, as she watched him fidget on her couch. He looked ready to attack her, but then he suddenly took a deep breath and rubbed his hands down his face.

"And how can you act like dreams don't matter. On Monday you were in tears because your dreams have been ending badly. Wasn't that the word you used, badly? I notice you're not crying over this one. Did it not end as *badly* as those others?"

Nada watched him a moment. She had no idea the cause of his irritation. Could it be that she had consensual sex with an animal in her dream, or that the animal had been a man where it mattered? His hands caressed her, and his erection penetrated her. Nada didn't admit she enjoyed it, and she was glad of it. Even though the sex dream hadn't been typical, she blushed enough just telling Grady about it. Remembering how badly it ended, she reached up to caress her shoulder. Although not wounded, she could still feel the pain as his razor sharp teeth sunk in. Nada didn't cry because the last dream didn't upset her as much as it terrified her. Until recently she never felt pain in her dreams, and the thought troubled her as she continued rubbing her shoulder.

"I didn't realize I was dreaming. I seemed comfortable with him and don't remember feeling fear, at least until he got rough with me. The pain of being bitten is what scared me the most."

"So this wasn't one of the dreams you were able to control?" He asked.

"Oh, hell no." She stammered with a nervous laugh. "Those have been bad enough, but this was different. I usually dream right after I go to sleep, since I will myself to it. This dream came to me in the middle of the night." She remembered the mountains. "The only things similar about this dream to my others are the mountains. They were in the last two dreams I had on purpose."

"Both those dreams went bad?"

She just nodded.

"How?" He asked gently.

Nada refused to get upset again. She kept her mind on the pain she felt to keep herself focused. "The mountains just appeared in them, and the person I was with began to *change*. It was sort of like what the panther and I did in the dream, but this was worse. What he *changed* into was…evil. It was like being thrown from Heaven and seeing the gates of Hell; especially the last time." She took a deep breath as she visualized the coat *morphing* into wings. That had been the strangest part. That and the strange voice she heard. Her arms being held in the painful grip of hands that began to *change* as well, but even that pain hadn't been nearly as severe as when the panther bit her shoulder.

A jolt flew through her as another memory assaulted her. A bite to the shoulder *was* how she had been infected. Yes, infected was a good word.

Grady noticed her reaction and moved closer. "What's wrong?"

She shook her head and blinked a few times. She wanted to remember what bit her, but the flicker of memory vanished. She knew dreams were symbolic and doubted that a -- she tried to think of a good word for a half man/half panther and came up with -- manther had actually infected her. The manther could be how she portrayed-- Her thoughts stopped there for a moment. If a man with her abilities infected her, and if he'd been like that for a long time, he would probably have the control needed to partially *change*, as Grady suggested.

Nada suddenly realized she didn't answer Grady. He patiently awaited her response, but she sensed his anxiety. She noticed his hand on her knee, and she covered it with one of her own. "I'm sorry, Grady. A bite to my shoulder is what made me as I am." Even as she said it, something wasn't right. She still missed a piece of the puzzle, so the memory wouldn't click into place. All she knew right then was that whatever infected her *had* bitten her shoulder.

Grady looked at her bare shoulder, visible due to the thin strap of her camisole. Of course, not seeing a scar didn't surprise him. "You just now remembered that?"

She nodded, blushing slightly. He continued looking at her shoulder, but she could almost tell by his expression what he thought. When he opened his mouth, she expected the worst and cringed.

"Were you bitten during sex?"

The question made perfect sense, she told herself, and it was the next logical step to make. She dreamt that she had sex and got bit on the shoulder. She then remembered that she had been bitten, so it would make sense that it happened during sex. The only problem with that logic was that she didn't think that's what happened. Of course, she didn't know for sure, but she had a feeling. Deep down she knew that she hadn't been having sex with what bit her.

Nada looked at Grady to study his face before responding. She doubted he would be upset by her lack of virginity in a normal woman. Her eyes widened by that thought. Up until then, she couldn't recall a time that she had sex, but she suddenly knew she wasn't a virgin. She could understand what Grady would be upset about. Had she had sex with an animal, while still being human on a conscious level? There was a name for people who did that, but how could she be grouped in that category? She couldn't be held accountable for acting like an animal, when she was an animal. Could she? Nada groaned and covered her mouth with her hands. Maybe she worried about nothing. She might have had sex anytime before her infection and just couldn't remember it. She could have had several boyfriends by the age of twenty-seven. She nodded and told herself not to immediately jump to any conclusions until she knew for sure.

"I don't remember." She replied. Her voice came out muffled, since her hands still covered her mouth. She dropped her hands and repeated what she said.

"Yet," he finished for her and nodded. "It's promising that you remembered that much. It might mean that all your memories will start to come back."

She wanted to say that she was glad, but the words wouldn't come. Did she really want to remember something her own mind had kept from her for just under three years? What if it was horrific? Of course, it would be nice to remember more of her life before her trip to Europe.  If she had a boyfriend, she'd like to remember him.

"Grady, are you married?"

The question obviously stunned him. "Am I married?" He repeated as a smile crept to his lips. "Yes, to my job." He waited a moment and smiled at her look of shock until the rest of his sentence registered. "Nada, would I have cooked you dinner, or accepted your dinner invitation tonight, if I was seriously involved with someone?"

Nada licked her lips and fidgeted in her seat. "If you didn't think of me as a threat to that relationship, yes." She responded frankly.

"Look in the mirror, Nada. Any other woman would be threatened by you hanging out with her husband."

"I'm not talking about other women. I'm talking about you." His comment about the mirror just clicked in her head, and her cheeks heated.

"Same difference. If I were married, I would have enough sense to know that my wife would feel threatened by you. Also, since I wouldn't be willing to explain your situation to her, I would not be able to spend so much time with you." He explained while leaning back into the couch.

"So if you did have someone, you wouldn't be helping me?" She asked, wishing the hurt wasn't so evident in her voice.

Grady leaned forward again and placed his elbows on his knees. "Oh, Nada, what am I going to do with you?" He asked in mock exasperation. "Of course, I would help you. Don't worry about another woman, all right? I'm not married, and I don't have a girlfriend. Besides the clinic, my dedication is to you right now. You have enough to deal with, so let me do the worrying, OK?"

"OK," she replied, sighing. *My dedication is to you,* echoed in her mind. "How are you going to help me control myself during a feed, so it doesn't always turn into a kill?"

Grady had a few ideas, but they all took place in his clinic, so they left Nada's apartment. She went in his car, so they could talk on the way, and she listened to what he had to say. One of the plans involved locking her inside a cage when she *changed* and giving her a bowl of blood. That reminded her of *changing* into the cat and doing the same thing, so she told him about how it had worked. The discovery pleased Grady, so she was glad she had told him. She didn't like the idea of being caged, but he informed her that he had a closet sized one so she would be free to move around. The next plan involved giving her a live animal and taking it away before she could drain its blood.

Nada gnawed on her lower lip when she heard that. "What if you get hurt? Isn't it dangerous to take food away from an animal?"

Grady nodded and glanced at her for a second. "Well, you said you're aware while you're *morphed*, so I'm counting on *you* not attacking me."

She winced slightly. "We'll have to practice with the bowl of blood first, that's for sure. I have to be able to control the animal instinct before I can trust that it won't attack you." She wouldn't be able to live with herself if she hurt Grady. "We'll also have to see if I can be in control with more aggressive animals than cats."

"That reminds me of something." He leaned over, opened the glove box and pointed to the contents. "There's a pad of paper in there. It would be helpful if I knew all the animals you can change into. Just write down as many as you can recall."

# Chapter Ten

Nada watched Grady through the bars of the cage. He had been right about it being roomy. She could even stand inside of it, though not amazing at her height, but Grady could as well. As she looked around, it felt as if she had been put in a jail cell. The door currently hung open, but how would she feel when he closed her inside? Her gaze settled on a metal chair in the center of the cage. Grady placed it there for her so she wouldn't have to sit on the floor, and she sat to wait while he documented everything in her chart. She found out after arriving at his clinic, that he started the chart on her after Fred brought her in as a wounded cat. As the silence continued, Nada became a bit nervous and looked at the floor. She noticed a folded towel next to the chair and wondered about it. She looked back at Grady and caught his frown. She bit her lip, wishing she hadn't given him that list.

Grady looked over all the different breeds. The number of animals she killed surprised him. He not only owed it to her to help learn control, but also to all the animals she might kill if he didn't. "Is this all of them?" He asked over his shoulder. When she didn't answer, he turned to look at her.

Nada thought about it for a moment and then shrugged. "That's all that I can think of right now." She looked down at her hands and began to mess with her cuticles to avoid eye contact. She still couldn't decide on how to tell him about the full moon, but she didn't have much longer before the next one would be upon her.

"Nada?"

She hesitated a few seconds after hearing his voice before looking up. She gave him a questioning look.

"Which animal would you like to try first?" He asked with a smile.

She sighed and shook her head. "Well, I've done the cat, but that doesn't mean it will work every time. Do you think I should try again, or try a different animal?"

He nodded as he thought about it. There was no reason to have her locked up just for her to turn into a cat. He looked at the list again and stopped on panther for a second before moving on, though that animal stayed with him. A cheetah was not one of the animals she provided, though both it and the panther were considered leopards. Of course, the cheetah sat on the bottom rung of that ladder, since it couldn't roar like all the other types of leopard. "Do you know for certain that you can change into a panther or did you write that because of your dream?"

Nada thought about it for a moment, before she nodded. "Maybe both." Her eyes widened as she groaned. Whatever made her *change* took over, and Nada closed her eyes as she quickly stripped off her clothes.

Grady watched in shock. "Nada, what are you doing? We didn't decide on a panther!" He realized his outburst fell on deaf ears. By the time Nada undressed, the black hair completely covered her body. Grady's mouth fell open as he noticed the open door. He raced across the room and gave the door a kick to shut it. When he heard the click of the latch, he turned back to Nada. He moved closer to watch the *morphing* from human to animal. He almost wished he had a camera but knew that wouldn't be a good idea.

"Holy shit!" Grady didn't normally curse, but it seemed justified in this instance. He doubted he'd ever get used to what he witnessed. Nada truly was a miracle. He thought about that for a second and wondered if he should have thought of it as a curse. He felt pretty certain that Nada saw it that way.

The panther circled the confines of the cage and growled. So far she avoided even looking at Grady. He moved a little closer to her and stopped about a foot away.

"Nada?" He asked in a low voice, but the panther continued to ignore him and circled her cramp quarters. The cage looked much smaller than it had when Nada's petite human body inhabited it. He repeated her name a little louder, but she still ignored him. His third attempt sharpened, and the panther swung on him. Her gold and black eyes locked with his, and he sucked in his breath. "Nada? Are you aware of me?"

Nada wanted to scream, not realizing that picturing a panther in her mind would turn her into one, even though she knew that's how it worked. She only sensed she could turn into a panther, since she'd never fed from one before. That dream had to mean something, but she couldn't really remember writing it on the list. She had no memory of ever being such a primitive, exotic animal before. She had awareness at the moment but couldn't get control of the panther.

At first she couldn't even recall where she was, but then she saw the bars of the cage and remembered. She circled the cage so close that her ribcage rubbed against the bars. She heard a voice but couldn't recognize it. She finally recognized Grady's voice and forced the animal to turn.

She looked into Grady's eyes, surprised how close he stood to the cage. *I've never killed a human before, and I never will,* she reminded herself or rather the animal she had become.

"Do you know me?" Grady tried again.

His voice echoed inside her head, and she growled. Though she knew him, she couldn't interpret his words. No human ever spoke to her while in animal form. The panther she became fought for control, but she knew she was stronger. She closed her eyes and concentrated. Grady repeated his question, and she sucked in her breath.

That time Nada understood him, but she didn't know how to let Grady know that. Could she make an animal nod? She again concentrated on controlling the panther, and it finally sat down. Since that was a non-aggressive move, she decided it would have to do.

Grady smiled and moved closer, and she moved back with a low growl. His eyebrows shot up at the response. If she had been human, Nada would have groaned. She didn't control what the animal thought. At that moment the *animal* visualized ripping out his jugular, but Nada wouldn't allow that. Her groan came out as a growl, and he moved back another foot.

Grady realized he dealt with a dangerous animal, and she may not be in full control. He had no idea how hard it was for her to get the panther to sit down. Grady would give himself a headache if he tried to put himself in her place. There was no way any human could empathize with what she had to go through. He nodded and moved back. The panther's chin came up a notch, and she returned to the bars.

"Alright, Nada, I get what you're telling me." He looked at her for a moment, admiring her shiny black coat. The cat also had a shiny coat of hair. Grady concluded that all the animals she turned into must be beautiful specimens. When she took their DNA, her body apparently filtered out all the impurities. He wished he could touch her. "Nada, try turning back into a human. Visualizing a panther made you *morph*, so just visualize your human form."

When she did nothing but return his stare, he stood and walked over to his mini-fridge, where he pulled out the container of blood. The microwave was in the other room, so he eyed the lock on the cage before leaving the lab. When he returned, Nada hadn't moved a muscle. When he approached, she licked her lips. Grady bit his lip.

"Nada, please move back a little, OK? I don't want to lose an arm." He was actually surprised when she did step back. He pushed the bowl through the opening at the bottom and then stepped back. As soon as he moved out of range, the panther attacked the bowl. Blood went everywhere. When she finished drinking the blood in the bowl, Nada began to lick what spilled on the floor.

Except for a few drops outside the cage, Grady didn't see any other blood when she finished. His hand moved up to cover his mouth as she circled the cage looking for more. A few minutes later, the panther crawled under the chair and curled its paws around the legs. Grady watched as she went to sleep. He moved closer to the cage and grasped the bars with both hands to watch the transformation. When the hair moved back into her body and her arms and legs began to stretch, he unlocked the cage door. Grady grabbed the towel and shook it. He looked at her a second longer before covering her naked body. Until his vision blurred, he hadn't even been aware of crying.

## Chapter Eleven

Grady sat on the floor next to Nada and watched her. He had no concept of time as he looked from her peaceful face to her arms and legs and then back to her face. He reached out and moved her dark hair aside before stroking a flushed cheek. He had no right to be upset about what he witnessed, since he put himself into the middle of it. He offered his help, and his help was what he needed to give. It just wouldn't be as easy as he hoped, but then nothing worth doing ever was.

Nada finally stirred and opened her eyes. Her gaze locked with a set of knees, and she moved her head so she could look up. Her eyes widened to see Grady sitting next to her. She looked down and grasped the towel across her body. She licked her dry lips and sat up. Nada had trouble meeting Grady's eyes. She looked around the cage and saw the upside down bowl next to the door. Tears filled her eyes as she remembered what transpired. She *changed* into a panther, and Grady hadn't been too happy about it. She looked back at him and shrugged.

"Sorry, I don't always decide." She licked her lips again and looked away. "At least not consciously," she muttered.

Grady looked at what he could see of her face. He fought the urge to move her hair aside and tilt her face to his. He bit his lip in frustration. Many times he watched his own patients die on the operating table. It almost killed him when he couldn't help an animal in need. He moved a hand to his mouth and looked away. His gaze caught her clothes, and he reached over to pick them up. Without looking at Nada, he placed them in her lap.

"Get dressed. I'll be in my office when you're ready." He then got up and left the cage.

Nada watched him walk away. She openly wept as she reached for her clothing. He would never help her now. If she couldn't even decide what kind of animal she *changed* into, how could she ever hope to control it?

Once dressed, she stood in the doorway to his office. The door was ajar, and Nada reached up, intending to tap on it. How could she face him? She knew she needed help, but would he still be willing to help her? She swallowed hard and knocked, the force pushing the door open farther. Grady looked up from behind his desk.

"Come on in."

Nada entered, smoothing her skirt as she walked nearer. When she got close to his desk, she sat without prompting but looked down.

Grady looked at the top of her head for a few moments. She went against everything he had ever known, but he couldn't fight how he felt about her. Though she scared him to death, he almost loved her. She could kill him without even trying, but he knew she wouldn't. Her strength excelled any man he knew, but he also knew she was more gentle than any animal he had ever encountered. Grady moved a hand across his right eye, trying to catch a tear before it formed. He never openly cried about anything, truly believing a man should never show such weakness, but Nada made him cry twice already tonight.

"Nada?" He finally found his voice. He needed to be the professional. She resembled a lost little girl in

Wonderland, but this Alice wouldn't have a happy ending.

She looked up with watery eyes. "Yes?"

Grady looked at her face and blinked a few times, before looking away for a moment. Her expressive face seemed so hopeful, that he hated to give her bad news. When he looked back, she still looked at him. "It's going to take a little longer than I had hoped."

Nada almost smiled with a relieved sigh. "How much longer *do* you think?"

He shook his head. "Could be a week or longer. We'll just have to wait and see. Don't you agree?" He countered. She could only shrug, but a smile crept to her lips. Grady almost felt reinforced by that smile. None so beautiful should ever be destined to suffer.

He nodded slowly. "It was good that we did this. We discovered something important."

Nada looked at him with a quizzical expression. "What's that?"

"We now know how you change. Whatever animal you picture in your mind is what you change into, right?"

Nada slowly nodded. "If I have fed on it, yes."

Grady's mind wandered for a moment, reminded of their conversation where he had asked her if she could *morph* into a human. Something about her responses bothered him, but he couldn't put his finger on it until right then. "Maybe you can't change into another person because you can't..." He paused to choose his words, surprised when Nada finished the sentence for him.

"Because I don't know what any of them look like?"

He slowly nodded. Nada's eyes misted, so she blinked a few times to clear them. She shook her head and shrugged. She opened her mouth to speak but had to clear her throat a few times before clearing the lump in her throat.

"Uh, I don't know how to answer that, and I don't really want to find out. It's bad enough that I can turn into animals. I don't really want to..." Nada couldn't finish the thought, instead drew in a shaky breath and shook her head. "I refuse to believe that it's possible."

Grady stared at her for a while. He couldn't fight the feeling of respect he had for her at that moment. She was such a little woman, but when she set her features in such a way, she seemed larger than life. If he were honest with himself, not to mention her, he had to admit that he didn't want her to be able to *morph* into other people. That would be beyond comprehension and more than he could handle. He nodded and took a deep breath. "OK, Nada. We have enough on our plate, don't we?" He watched as her hard look transformed to a grateful smile, and his newly discovered love for her grew.

They had both been tired, so Nada agreed to come back after work the next night. The following afternoon at the hospital she stared off into space, and a familiar voice intruded her thoughts.

"You look like you just lost your last friend."

Nada looked at Dr. Thorton and tried to smile. He was at his most charming when he smiled, so it was hard to not return the expression. She couldn't keep her thoughts away from the night before. The last thing she wanted to do was disappoint Grady. "I'm sorry, Dr. Thorton. I didn't mean to ignore you. Had you asked me something?"

He shook his head and frowned. "No, *Nurse Berch*, I only said that one thing. I would hate to think you *could* ignore me." He added and placed a hand to his chest. Nada finally smiled, relieved that he lifted her spirits.

"Not you, Dr. Thorton." She replied with a laugh. If she could ignore him, the other nurses would think that she had something wrong with her. He was entirely too attractive not to notice, but then he knew that. Fortunately, he didn't let it go to his head. Nada always thought he just enjoyed the attention, and there wasn't anything wrong with that.

Zack relaxed and leaned against the counter. "That's good. I haven't seen much of you lately, at least since the party. I'm sorry you had to leave so early. I was hoping we could dance."

"Well, we've both been very busy.  Maybe there will be another party soon." She replied, avoiding his gaze. She filled in some of her paperwork, to give her hands something to do.  She sensed Zack moving closer over the counter. She looked up and watched him lean forward to place his chin on his hands, which were on the side of the counter closest to her.

"What is it about me that you don't like, Nada?"

She looked into his eyes and sighed. He really was a nice man, and she hated for him to get the wrong impression.  "I like you, Zack.  I'm just—"

He interrupted her, "Aha, I knew you could call me by my first name at work, if you wanted to." He gave her a beaming smile, which caused her to blush. She returned his smile with a half-hearted glare.

"You caught me off guard, Dr. Thorton. I'm sure it won't happen again." She averted her gaze. He always had a way of making her feel like a teenager. He was just too good looking.  She preferred Grady's looks, which always made her feel warm and womanly. Thinking of Grady reminded her of what they would be working on that night. She hoped it went better than their first attempt. Nada looked back at Zack. "I'm sorry, was there something you need me to do for you?" She asked, wishing she could stop thinking of both men at the same time.

Zack's gaze lowered for an instant before moving back up to her mouth. His gaze lingered there before he looked into her eyes. "You mean professionally?"

She sucked in her breath and nodded, all the while hoping her cheeks weren't as flushed as they felt.

He pushed himself away from the counter and straightened to his full height. Nada tilted her head back to keep eye contact. "Nah, I was just on my way out and thought I'd say hi. And of course my day isn't complete until I've made you blush. You're just so damn cute with a little color in your cheeks."

Nada reached up and covered her cheeks with both hands. She would never admit it to him, but she did enjoy his teasing. The flirting wasn't so bad either, but she didn't want him to take anything too seriously. "I hope I'm not the only one you like to make blush."

"No, but you're the most fun. Why do you think I keep trying for that date?" He lightly tapped the counter. "Well, I've taken you away from your work long enough. I'll see you later, Nada Berch."

"Have a good evening, Dr. Thorton." She watched him walk down the long corridor and noted his sexy gait. She suddenly wondered about Grady's walk, since she hadn't noticed. Nada chuckled and shook her head. It wouldn't do her any good to let her thoughts go anywhere with either man. Though better off on her own, she felt it much nicer to finally have someone to talk to. The previous night may not have gone well, but Nada looked forward to spending more time with Grady. He was determined to help her, and for that she would be eternally grateful.

She drove to his clinic directly from the hospital, though she did stop for take out. They would be busy the whole night and would need food. By the time she got to the clinic, Margaret had already gone home. The lights were off, but Grady left the front door unlocked for her. She walked through the reception area and headed for the lab.  The door was ajar, so she pushed it open. When she saw Grady, she froze in the threshold.

He bent over the sink and squeezed water from the washcloth in his hand.  Nada watched the water run from his shoulder down his right arm, and her eyes were drawn to the flexed bicep in his left arm. She pulled in a ragged breath and discarded any thought of him not being as sexy as Zack Thorton. Without even realizing it, she moved closer. Her gaze lingered on the muscles across his naked back before moving to his ribcage. As she neared him, she focused on every water droplet and licked her suddenly dry lips.

Grady sighed as he continued to rinse the soap away.  He wished he had the time to go home and shower, but he expected Nada soon. A neighbor's dog attacked one of his patients and got blood all over him. He certainly didn't want to deal with that all night, so he was glad he always kept a change of clothes at the clinic.

He dropped the washcloth into the sink and reached for the towel. As he dried his chest and arms, he looked down to make sure his pants hadn't gotten wet. He saw something out of the corner of his eye and turned sharply, sucking in his breath. Nada stood less than ten feet away and clutched a white bag in her hands. Her knuckles were almost as white as the bag.

"Oh, I didn't hear you come in." He said as he looked up to her face. His eyes widened as he realized she stared at his chest. He looked down at the water droplets and began to dry them away. When he looked back at Nada, she met his gaze. "Are you OK?"

Nada nodded and swallowed hard, trying to come to grips with her feelings. She gave plenty of sponge baths to patients in the past, so why would Grady's naked chest affect her so much? Had she gotten so used to thinking of him as a doctor, that she didn't realize there was a well-built male body under that white lab coat? Just a few hours earlier, she had wondered if he had a sexy walk. She realized then that she never noticed before. It was only after noticing Zack that the thought even crossed her mind.

"Nada?" Grady's voice interrupted her musings.

Although she looked at him, she finally focused on his face. "Yes?"

Grady finished drying off and pulled on a shirt. "I'm sorry you walked in on that. I didn't expect you for at least another fifteen minutes. Traffic must have been light?"

Nada shook her head and looked at what she held. She released the tight grip on the bag and placed it on the counter in front of her. "Don't worry about it. It isn't as if I haven't seen an undressed man before." She pointed to the bag. "I got us something to eat."

He walked over to her and looked into the bag. Nada closed her eyes as his clean damp scent hit her. She bit her lower lip and took a slow deep breath. Grady reached in and pulled out a burger.

"Thanks, I'm starving." He replied and moved across the room.

"Hey, I owe you so much for helping me, it was the least I could do." She reached in and pulled out her sandwich. She placed it on the counter and filled a glass with water. She drank the entire glassful before turning toward Grady. "So, what do you have planned for tonight?"

At first he could only stare at her and blink. He had a lot of experience with women and animals, so he knew a sexual look when he saw one. He just couldn't be sure which part of Nada had been attracted to him. Since she obviously didn't want to talk about it, he let it go. She had merely been surprised to see him partially undressed. He nodded, trying to convince himself that was all it had been. "We'll stick with blood in a dish, until you are able to gain control every time. After that, you'll go to the next step."

"What's the next step, live animals?" She asked and took a bite from her sandwich.

"We can deal with that when we get there. I just want you to focus on one thing at a time."

Nada nodded and ate her last bite of sandwich. She then took off her sweater and placed it and her purse on the counter. "I'm ready when you are."

By the end of that week, Nada could control the animal she had *changed* into. It took a lot of will power, but she could to do it. She didn't know for sure if that was due to her need not to kill the animals she fed upon, or to change the disapproving look in Grady's eyes. She never wanted to see that lost look in his eyes again. He was the one person she could trust with her secret, and she didn't know what she would do if she lost him.  He truly held her life in his hands.

They talked quite a bit during their week together. He asked many questions of her and curiously asked about her job, since she had access to blood. She finally admitted to being a nurse at the local hospital. She didn't remember going to college, but she found her transcript from a junior college back home. She then decided to get her nursing degree, which she earned less than three months earlier. While she earned her degree, she interned at the local hospital. She discovered the wisdom of working with blood over two years earlier while volunteering at the hospital. When she officially became a nurse, she moved and found her current nursing job.

Grady himself was new to their city. His veterinarian clinic opened less than two months earlier, and Nada moved there about a month before that. His mind pondered the connection before discarding it. It was just a coincidence, after all.  Maybe there *was* a preordained reason for them meeting, but he wouldn't concern himself with that. Before he met Nada, he didn't even believe in vampires and werewolves. He would definitely have to reevaluate those opinions. Nada's origin could only be in some fantasy or science fiction book. When Grady looked at her, he remembered how beautiful he thought her upon their first meeting. Though still just as beautiful, she certainly couldn't be considered a fantasy. She made up most nightmares, even her own.

Nada arrived at the clinic early on Friday morning. Their experiment progressed well, and she was more hopeful than she had been when they first started. She didn't find Grady in his office when she walked in, so she walked back through the lab and heard his voice. It came from a room in the back of the clinic. She never walked back there and didn't know what it was. She stopped in the threshold when she saw Grady. He stood in front of a row of cages, and Nada's gaze went from one cage to the next. A cat laid in one, a puppy in another, and a rabbit sat in the one directly in front of Grady. The cat and the puppy were asleep, but the rabbit's eyes locked on her. Grady must have sensed her presence, since he turned toward her.

"Good morning." He smiled at her and approached.

"Hi." She pointed to the cages. "Patients?" She asked.

"Mostly," he nodded. "The rabbit's for you."

She cocked her head to the side, as if she hadn't heard him right. "Excuse me?"

"You've done well this past week. I think it's time to move to step two."

Nada looked at the rabbit and watched its nose twitch. She felt her heart race and shook her head. "I don't know if I'm ready for that, yet."

"There's only one way to find out. You didn't *feed* this morning, did you?"

She looked at Grady and shook her head, since she knew he didn't mean breakfast. "It's harder for me to *change* if I had." She looked at the rabbit again, trying to decide which animal she would choose. Nada wondered if Grady got the rabbit since he knew she never fed on one before. She would soon be able to add it to her list of choices. She would soon be quite the chameleon.

Nada waited in the cage and looked at the opened door. Grady would close it once he and the rabbit were inside with her. She glanced up when she heard him approach and fought the smile at his appearance. He wore a layered body suit, which covered him from neck to crotch. Only his denim-clad legs were unprotected, since he wore a mesh mask over his face and head.

"I see you're not taking any chances." Her hand covered her mouth to hide the smile. Her expression grew serious when she focused on the rabbit in his arms. Nada backed into a corner as they entered the cage, and Grady closed the door behind him.

"Of course not. You've done well, but I have to leave room for mistakes. Just don't turn into anything too aggressive, OK?" He thought of the panther but didn't dare voice the word for fear her subconscious would choose for her.

Nada nodded and watched him place the rabbit on the floor. She watched it scurry around, looking for the exit. The headache started a few minutes earlier, and her temple throbbed. She looked back at Grady, who stared at her. Their eyes locked on each other, and time seemed to stand still. Nada's breathing quickened, and her heart raced. She reached up and began to unbutton her blouse, but Grady's gaze never left her face.

Grady couldn't look away. He wanted to watch her eyes *change*. He saw her body *morph* plenty of times, but he never watched her eyes. He sucked in his breath as the color lightened from brown to gold and her pupils stretched to slits. As her body compacted within itself, Grady had to crouch down to keep eye contact. The eyes grew smaller and the lids became darker as reddish-brown hair covered them. Grady finally looked at the rest of the face and saw the pointy snout of the fox she turned into. Her bushy tail cut the air behind her as she moved it back and forth.

"Take control, Nada." He told her as he backed up a little. He needed to be ready to take the rabbit from her, so he got down on both knees.

Nada looked from Grady to the rabbit. It made terrified little squeaks as it tried to squeeze through the small opening at the bottom of the door. She pounced on it in an instant. Grady fought the impulse to grab the rabbit and protect it. He watched as Nada sunk her teeth into the back of its neck.

"Only take what you need, Nada. Nada...Nada." He kept repeating her name, so she would know who she was. The rabbit began to shake its back legs. "Nada, stop!" He shook his head, realizing he couldn't wait any longer. He went to grab the rabbit, and Nada turned on him. She bared her bloody fangs at him and growled. Grady pushed her away with one gloved hand and reached for the rabbit.

The fox tensed to jump on Grady, but Nada fought for control and finally won. While she had it, she visualized her human body.

Grady didn't spare Nada a glance, as he opened the door to the cage and ran for the operating table. Everything had been laid out in preparation, so he didn't notice Nada changing back. Once she completed her transition into a human, she sat back on her heels and watched Grady applying the sutures to the rabbit's neck. When he finished, he checked its vitals. Grady sighed as he realized he saved it in time. He ran the back of his hand across his forehead and tossed everything into the sanitizer. He then picked up his new patient and carried the rabbit back to its cage.

The first thing he noticed when he returned to the lab was Nada still sitting on her heels inside the cage. She stared at the floor, and he followed her gaze. Some of the rabbit's blood spilled there.

"Nada?"

She looked up at him with tears in her eyes. "That's the first time I was able to make myself *change* back."

Grady found it hard to concentrate on what she said and took a deep breath. "Did you forget to get dressed?"

She looked down at her naked body and shrugged. "We humans are the only animals that wear clothes. Modesty is really stupid, don't you think?" She asked as she reached for her blouse. "I'm sorry, Grady." She told him without looking at him.

Grady knew she didn't apologize for not getting dressed, but he decided to humor her. "Hey, there's nothing wrong with seeing a naked woman."

Nada looked at him and smiled. "That's not what I meant."

"I know, but it made you smile." He watched her stand and approach. "Don't be sorry about anything. I'm proud of what you've accomplished this week. I didn't expect it to be perfect the first try. Nothing ever is."

She nodded and placed a hand on the metal table. She wanted to impress him and hated the disappointment she could hear in his voice. "Will it be alright?" She asked and looked toward the patient ward.

"He'll be fine."

Nada nodded and swallowed the lump in her throat. She looked back at the table and traced a figure eight on its surface. She was hardly conscious of the act but had to do something to avoid looking at Grady. "I heard something once. I can't remember where or when it was, but it has stayed with me." She paused to clear her throat. "Though we cannot control the length of our lives, we *can* influence the width and depth. The width is the amount of people we touch during our lives, and the depth is how many of those people that we loved."

Nada bit her lower lip as she felt her eyes mist. She closed them for a moment and swallowed hard. After licking her dry lips, she finally looked at Grady. "Will I ever be able to say I had such width or depth in my life?" Her voice cracked on the last word, and she looked away.

Grady could only stare at her, and he watched as a stray tear slowly rolled down her cheek.

## Chapter Twelve

She walked in the forest. Without looking, she knew she *morphed* into a panther and that mountains were behind her. Looking up at the full moon, she walked to a clearing and stopped in the center. She sat and waited, but the voice surprised her.

*Είστε έτοιμοι για με?*

She turned her head to look around, eyes widening upon hearing the strange voice again.

*Who's there?* She called out. When the voice repeated the question, she looked toward the trees. *I can't understand. Where are you?*

*Συμπύκνωση.*

Nada shook her head and tried to focus on the darkness between the trees. At first she didn't see anything, but then she saw him among the trees in front of her. The black panther emerged from the darkness and approached her. She waited for him to partially change into a man, but it didn't happen. *What?*

*I said 'concentrate'*, he said in the same language, but she finally understood.

How could an animal speak to her?

*Because I don't have to speak for you to hear me,* he answered.

She then realized his voice was only in her head, and that she had been responding to him without speaking out loud. They could read each other's minds.

*Who are you?* She asked him, suddenly realizing that his earlier question had been *'Are you ready for me?'* She didn't want to ask 'ready for what?'

*Don't you know, yet?* He responded.

*Should I?* She countered.

The panther stopped directly in front of her and looked up. She followed his gaze, and they both stared at the full moon.

*At least you haven't been dreaming of* him *lately.*

She almost asked who he meant but then realized he spoke of her dream lover vampire. Was he the reason her dreams had gone so badly? How could *he* manipulate her dreams?

*You were there?* Just as she asked it, she could almost hear him hissing *why are you dreaming of him?* The voice had been the same, though she hadn't understood what he said at the time. Now she knew what had happened to her dreams.

He stared at her for a few moments. *I've been watching you for a while,* he finally responded.

*What's your name?* She pressed.

He looked back at her. *I'm not known by any name, though you can call me Kyros.*

Nada stared at the animal face in front of her. Was he a human like her? She wanted to know what he looked like, in order to determine whether or not she knew him. She looked down at her paws and visualized her human hands. As she began to *change*, she pushed up onto her hind legs. They stretched and reformed into her human legs. When she stood before him as a human, the panther stared up at her. She stared down at him and raised her eyebrows.

"Can you do that, Kyros?" She challenged him.

*You know I can, my love, but it's not time for that, yet. You have one more week before we meet again. Have you missed me?*

"Missed you?" She asked. "I don't even know you."

He gave her an intense look before gazing back at the full moon. He then looked at her and reached out one paw. She watched as it alone *changed* into a human hand. He caressed her cheek for a moment and then lowered his hand to slide one finger along her breast. As she watched his hand return to the paw, she covered her bare breasts with her arms. Strange that she forgot about her nakedness, since he obviously hadn't. He then turned to walk away. Right before he reached the woods, he turned to look over his shoulder.

*I have a special birthday present in store for you, my dear. I look forward to mating with you for real.* He let out a soft growl before disappearing through the trees.

"That was just a dream," she said under her breath.

*No, it wasn't,* his voice answered, *and neither is this.*

Nada jolted awake and sat up. She swallowed hard as she tried to catch her breath. The dream wasn't as bad as her first one, but in some ways it had been worse. She threw back the sheet and ran for the kitchen, flipping on the light to look at the calendar. She never paid any attention to her birthdays. They always came and went, since she never had anyone to celebrate with. Nada looked at the 13th of October and sucked in her breath. Not only was her birthday during a full moon, it was also Friday the 13th. Her hand went to her throat as she thought about the symbolic nature of her 30th birthday coinciding with a full moon thirty days after the last one, and occurring on Friday the 13th. Adding her strange dreams into the mix made her very nervous indeed. Her birthday and the next full moon were exactly one week away.

## Chapter Thirteen

Nada decided the time had come to tell Grady about the full moon. She worked Friday night and all day Saturday, so now the full moon was only five days away, and she hadn't been able to stop thinking about Kyros. She kept trying to convince herself that he couldn't be real but wasn't quite succeeding. Every full moon for almost three years, she couldn't control or even know what she did. Her thoughts kept returning to the large cage in Grady's clinic. He could monitor what she did and then let her know the next morning. The more she thought about it over the weekend, the more she liked the idea. She called him Sunday morning and asked to see him as soon as possible.

"I can be at your place in less than an hour." He told her.

"That's great."

"Nada, what's wrong?" He finally asked.

"I'd rather tell you this to your face," she replied.

Grady groaned. "That bad, huh?"

Nada didn't speak for a moment. "I'll see you soon."

"I'll leave right now." He hung up without saying another word.

She stared at the phone for a moment and smiled.

Just over fifteen minutes later she heard a knock at the door. Nada stopped about a foot short of opening it.

She bit her lip and rested her hand on the knob. After the second impatient knock, she finally opened the door.

When Grady's eyes locked on her, he spread out his arms and shrugged. "Well?"

"Come on in," she replied and stepped aside.

"Nada, the suspense is killing me." He grabbed her hand and pulled her to the couch with him. "What is it?"

Once seated, Nada turned to face Grady. She took a deep breath and let it out slowly. "I haven't told you everything about my...situation."

Grady merely nodded, which shocked Nada speechless for a few moments. She expected surprise not acceptance. "Uh, it has to do with this Friday night."

Grady's mind raced as he tried to think of anything of significance that would be happening that night. "The full moon?"

Nada blinked and then blinked again, before slowly nodding. First he showed no surprise that she held something back, and then he immediately targeted the full moon. "What do you know?"

Grady shook his head at her suspicious tone. "Relax, Nada. You can change into animals, which has always made me think of a werewolf, which reminds me of the full moon. It follows, that's all. Now, I just need you to tell me what's special about it."

Nada nodded and sighed. "OK, when I first got back from Europe, it took a few months before I realized what was going on. I didn't even know I could *change,* because it happened when I wasn't aware of it. My body took over, when it needed the blood badly enough. I went through several full moons and wasn't even aware they were any different than any other night."

She stopped for a moment to gather her thoughts. Grady's expression grew puzzled, but he didn't speak.

"Back then, it took a few months before I could remember what I did after I *changed*. Then I started realizing that I didn't have all the memories." She took a deep breath and finished in a rush. "I never retain any memories of what I do during a full moon."

Grady let that sink in before speaking. "Even as time has gone by and you are aware while you're an animal, you still don't..." He stopped talking as Nada began to nod.

Before he could say anything else, she continued with her idea. "Before now I've never had anyone I could trust with this. I'd like to be in the cage this Friday night. You can let me know what happens."

Several werewolf movies flashed through Grady's mind. Folklore always had werewolves killing humans or having them changed into more werewolves. He couldn't decide if Nada was more like a vampire or a werewolf, or could she be the first hybrid? If that were true, then she was a hybrid of two myths. His mind tried to be intellectual about the newest information it had just been given, but it was definitely between a rock and a hard place. He knew so much about animals, but could any of that be applied to Nada? He searched his knowledge for logical conclusions to make regarding the full moon. The moon affected several things. A woman's reproductive cycle centered on one, as well as the tides. His mind searched for a third possibility, but reproduction stayed with him.

Grady looked back at Nada. She was a woman, and he never thought to ask her any personal questions. "Do you menstruate?" He asked quickly.

Nada's eyes flew open with surprise. "Well, I don't have a normal cycle."

"What do you mean?" He would hold off on making any conclusions until Saturday, but he didn't want to blindly go into Friday night.

Nada blushed. "The night before the full moon I begin to bleed, but it's pretty mild. The worst part is I swell and get a little crampy. It's all cleared up the day after full moon."

"So you have a two day period?"

She nodded but didn't add anything else. Nada knew about a human female's reproductive cycle, but Grady doubted she knew much about an animal's estrous cycle. Without actually examining her the night before the full moon, he wouldn't be able to tell if she went into "heat." Of course, he knew that estrous couldn't be completed in only two days. It usually lasted two to three weeks. He then remembered how her body could repair itself when she changed from human to animal and then back to human. Did the *morphing* speed everything up? "God!" He muttered under his breath and looked at Nada. "There's no other time you bleed?"

She shook her head. "I always thought it was due to needing blood all the time. I didn't think my body could spare any. What are you thinking?" She finally asked.

Grady's hand moved up to cover his mouth as he stared at her. He looked from her eyes to her nose and then mouth and chin. Her flawless skin was so breathtaking, and he doubted she'd ever had any trouble with acne as a teenager. Then again, her appearance could be a side effect of having incredible regenerative abilities. "I'm thinking that it's a good idea that you be caged on Friday night. I have a suggestion of my own, though. Would you have any objection to being examined the night before?"

"Examined?"

"I need to do a pelvic exam." He almost smiled as her eyes widened again. "Though it would probably make more sense if you changed into an animal first. I would then know exactly what I was looking for, and it might make it easier on us both."

"Could you do a regular pelvic on me as a human?" She asked quietly. "Maybe you could do both?"

Grady opened his mouth but closed it. He had been afraid she'd be offended. "You mean do I have the medical knowledge?" When she nodded, he continued. "I went to medical school. I even interned, but I couldn't handle the pressure or the stress. I've always loved animals, so that seemed the logical change. Being a vet was the best decision I ever made. Of course, my internship was years ago, but I'm pretty sure I can remember how a pelvic is done."

He didn't add that it probably wouldn't uncover anything about an estrous cycle, but then again it could. Considering how she bent all the rules of science, he couldn't wait to take a look. "How long has it been since your last exam?" He asked, already knowing the answer.

"All I know is that it was before all *this*."

"Sounds like a plan then. I can examine you first, and then you can change into a cat. I'll then do another examination. It will give you another chance to change back without feeding." They worked on her learning control, and all the while she knew that she had no control over herself during a full moon. He tried not to be bitter about her withholding that information from him, but he felt a little hurt. "I wish you had told me all this weeks ago, Nada."

"I know, and I'm sorry. I just felt you had enough to deal with. I always intended to tell you," she offered.

He nodded and cleared his throat. "Well, all this talking has worked up an appetite. You hungry?"

It was late when Grady finally left. Nada leaned against the door after she closed it. Once they decided to have dinner, they discussed nothing further about the full moon. Nada knew that Grady wanted to change the subject, and that not trusting him with the information sooner had hurt him. She poured them both a glass of wine to help them relax.

She tilted her head back and looked up. She thoroughly enjoyed his company and opened up about how her life had been the last three years. She hadn't even realized how tight the lid was on her feelings, but it started to open. With that realization, she began to feel quite fond of Grady. He made her feel so comfortable, that she knew she could tell him anything. She smiled as she replayed some of their conversation in her mind.

"Has there ever been anyone special in your life?" He had asked her.

Nada looked down and ran her finger around the rim of her glass. She shrugged. "I can't remember. I know there hasn't been anyone since Europe. How could there be?" Against her will, her eyes misted over. She turned away and ran a hand over her face. She felt his warm hand on her shoulder and leaned her cheek against it. Clearing her throat, she looked back at him and smiled. "It hasn't all been bad. Until recently, I've been special in my dreams."

He looked sad at first but then smiled. His smile turned to a soft chuckle. He surprised them both by hugging her. "You're special all the time to me."

As they separated, the strongest impulse to kiss him surged through her, but Nada looked down instead. She pulled away a little more before she trusted herself to meet his gaze again. As she looked into his smiling face, she wondered if her fantasies could drag *him* into her dreams. Would she want to take the chance?

She still thought of that as she closed the door behind him. She wondered if she could do it without a picture, since she always used the poster. Nada got ready for bed and then got under the covers. She stared up at the ceiling, trying to visualize Grady's face above her. Realizing she could do the same thing without staring up, she closed her eyes. She took a deep breath as she then visualized them kissing. She sighed as she drifted off.

They were in a room lit only by candles, that surrounded the bed she lounged on, but Nada had eyes only for Grady. His hair was wet, and she'd been right about it being curly. She reached out and touched one of the curls.

"Why do you straighten this?" She asked in wonder. She then noticed that the rest of him was wet and sighed a shaky breath. The only thing he wore was a pair of black shorts. She ran her other hand down the muscles in his chest. "Oh my, why do you wear clothes?"

She didn't blush at such open questions, since this was her dream. Of course, Grady willingly played along.

"Do you want me to take them off?" He asked as he leaned forward to kiss her jaw.

"Oh yeah," she breathed. As their lips were about to meet, she heard something. She peered over his shoulder and looked around. "Did you hear that?"

Grady didn't answer and Nada looked beyond the candles. Her eyes focused on the walls, only to discover they weren't in a room but a cave. She looked for the opening and found it behind her. She turned to face it and got off the bed. She picked up one of the candles and walked toward it. Remembering Grady, she turned to ask him to go with her, but both he and the bed were gone. She stood alone in the cave. This was not supposed to be part of her fantasy.

Taking a deep breath, Nada wondered if she should make herself wake up. Did she really want to see what was at the end of that tunnel? Deciding to face her fears, she walked forward. Luckily for her, her short height didn't hinder her as the tunnel narrowed the further she walked. The candle flickered, and she held up her hand to protect it. Holding her breath, she bit her lip until the flame stopped dancing on the wick. She then continued walking. The noise got louder, and Nada became nervous. She did not like the unknown, and she could not identify what she heard.

She could tell she neared the end of the tunnel and bent over a little to get through. As she straightened to look around the huge cavern, the voice behind her startled her.

"So, where are we now, Sunshine?"

Nada spun around and came face to face with her favorite vampire. She gasped, "What are *you* doing here?"

He shrugged his black clad shoulders. "I guess your subconscious felt I would be more useful to you here than your very human boyfriend. Don't you want me around anymore? I thought you loved me."

Nada narrowed her eyes and took a step back. She doubted her subconscious sent him, since she didn't think he would talk to her that way. The noise suddenly got very strong, and she realized too late that he was sent to distract her. She spun around and dropped the candle. In the mere second it took before the light went out, she saw something flying at her with its arms outstretched in front of it. Even with her exceptional eyesight, she couldn't see much after that. The winged beast grabbed her arms and lifted her off the ground. Its claws dug into her flesh as she struggled. Nada opened her mouth to scream and...

...woke up. She practically flew out of the bed, thinking the beast was still after her. As she pressed herself against her wall and attempted to slow her wild breathing, she was relieved she hadn't screamed that time. She now believed it possible to be too scared to scream. What the hell had grabbed her? She never saw anything like it before. As she thought about it, what little she saw of it already started to fade. The only things that remained, as her breathing returned to normal, were the colors black and red. She didn't even try to sort out whether that was the creature itself or just the wings, since they spanned the entire cavern. Nada sank down to the floor and hugged her knees. "What the hell is going on?"

The empty room did not answer.

The next day, she stood at her living room window, sipping coffee from a mug. Even though she looked outside that was not what she saw. The creature from her nightmare plagued her. Nada sighed and turned away from the window. Her gaze touched on the sketchpad, and she reached for it. Picking up the pencil with her other hand, she closed her eyes. She forced her mind to remember what the winged beast looked like and touched the tip of the pencil to paper. The wings shown clear in her mind, but everything else was a dark blur. When Nada opened her eyes and focused on the paper, she gasped and dropped the sketchpad. Her hand slowly moved up to cover her gaping mouth as the pencil slipped from the limp fingers of her other hand. She hadn't even been aware she drew it, but there it was. The face hid in shadows, but the glowing eyes were clear. The enormous wings spread wide, as were the muscled arms and taloned claws. Nada hadn't turned the page, so she finished her park scene by having the creature descend on the couple embracing on the bench.

## Chapter Fourteen

It was late Thursday evening and Grady sat at his desk. Nada slept in her cage in the other room. She arrived shortly after his clinic closed and he performed the pelvic on her first as planned. After she *morphed* into the cat, he put her to sleep for the second exam. Since he couldn't send any samples to the lab, he was at a disadvantage on his findings. He waited to draw any conclusions until after both exams were complete. He hadn't been surprised to discover that the cat was in heat. That she already neared the end of the proestrus stage did surprise him, since according to Nada she began bleeding that afternoon.

Grady looked over the notes he took during both exams. He felt relief when he saw everything where it should be in her human body, though her menstrual cycle was no longer normal. Her body was not sloughing the uterine lining but instead prepared for ovulation. He was so absorbed in the notes, that he didn't even notice Nada walking into his office. She stood in front of his desk, waiting for him to look up.

Nada leaned forward and tried to read what was in front of Grady, but she couldn't read his handwriting upside down. When he still didn't look up, she cleared her throat. He glanced up sharply.

"I had no trouble changing back," she said to break the silence.

"That's no surprise. We've been practicing for weeks." He looked back at the notes. "Have a seat, Nada."

"Am I OK?" She asked nervously.

Grady looked at her worried face. He looked from one feature to the next; trying to assure himself that nothing was different. If her reproductive system could evolve into something else, what would be next? "You're in perfect health, Nada, but..." He had trouble going on. How could he put into words what was going through his mind? He saw the question in her expression, but she remained silent. He nodded reassuringly. "You're in heat," he said simply.

Nada swallowed hard and moved a hand up to her mouth. "Animals go into heat, Grady, not humans," she replied through her fingers.

"Well, you have a lot of animal in you now, Nada. I'm curious to see what happens tomorrow night, but I think it all revolves around the full moon. I think that is the one night a month that you can mate." He tried not to think what that meant, but he couldn't ignore it. "I'm assuming that you've never been pregnant? At least to your knowledge?"

She shook her head.

"You've been..." Grady paused to search for the right word to describe her situation but couldn't quite find it. He settled on "...special...for almost three years. I find it hard to believe that you've mated about thirty times and never conceived. I don't care how fast your system works, there's no way you could..." He stopped since he almost said there was no way she could have a litter within one night. "You've never cramped or had break-through bleeding or anything like that?"

"You're asking me if I could have aborted and not known it? I'm a nurse, Grady. I think I would know if I were pregnant." She scowled but then smiled.

"What's funny?" Grady asked with a smile of his own.

She shook her head. "It's not funny, really, I just got this mental image of all these aroused animals standing in line, waiting for their turn." She shook her head, again. "I just don't think that's what has been going on. There's something special about this full moon. I never dreamt of Kyros before. He specifically told me that he had something planned for us tomorrow. I don't know much about an animal's heat, but is it possible that I go into heat but don't mate?"

Grady thought about it for a moment and slowly nodded. "Some animals only mate once a year, and others will wait until they meet their life mate. Right now, you're in the proestrus stage. That means you're body is getting ready for the estrus stage, where mating is possible. While in the proestrus stage, the female will attract males but will reject all advances. Since I don't know the kind of animal that made you the way you are, it could be possible that until your intended mate is with you, you'll stay in the proestrus stage until the heat is complete. I don't know of any animal that does that, but it would explain why you've never been pregnant. Going by that assumption, you change during the full moon, are in heat, but reject any male that advances. You might even have killed them."

That rang so true that Nada got chills. She rubbed her arms and closed her eyes. "Is Kyros my mate?"

Grady shrugged. "This is out of my league, Nada." Although it took her saying the name twice, Grady just realized she gave the manther a name. "Kyros? Did you remember that name?"

"No, I guess I forgot to tell you that I dreamt of him last Friday. He told me that he didn't have a name, but that I could call him Kyros." She debated on telling Grady of her dream of the winged creature but decided against it. Not only did she not want to tell him how that dream started, but it still terrified her to even think of it let alone talk about it. It couldn't have anything to do with her, so she didn't see the need to tell him.

Grady's thoughts went back to college and the time he spent with his fraternity. He heard that name before, and it then clicked in his mind. "Kyros is Greek for master."

Nada felt a chill and wrapped her arms about herself. "Why wouldn't he have a real name?"

Grady shook his head. "Did you two only talk in this dream?"

"Yes, he told me that he had something special planned for my birthday. He said he was looking forward to meeting me again and mating with me for real." She rubbed her hands up and down her arms.

"Was he a man or a panther, or a combination again?"

"Just a panther. He did *change* one paw to a hand and stroked my face, but that was it."

Grady watched her for a moment. He could tell she was very uncomfortable with the topic. Kyros understandably made her nervous. "It was this last dream that made you want to be locked up tomorrow night?"

She nodded. "And that was before I found out he's my master. Or rather, he thinks he's my master, right? God, is he who I've been waiting for?" Her lower lip quivered at the question.

"If he exists, then he could be just like you. It would make sense that he is your intended." He ground his teeth together at the thought. "He may even have been the one that infected you. Makes sense, doesn't it?"

Nada nodded. "He does exist, Grady. It's unfortunate but true, and why has he waited so long to contact me?"

"Maybe the planets had to align." He meant it to sound funny, or even sarcastic, but didn't succeed at either. "Your age might have something to do with it. Or maybe some amount of time had to pass before you were ready for him. Until you meet him, you'll never know."

"Yeah, and the idea of meeting him terrifies me. I'm glad I'll be locked up." She looked up with tears in her eyes. "I'd hate to think of where I'd be if I hadn't met you when I did."

Grady slowly nodded. "Speaking of tomorrow, do you lose the entire day or just the night?"

Nada forced herself to stop thinking of Kyros and focus on the question asked. "Just the night, and you can't set your watch by it, but it's always close to 10:00. I guess the full moon is at its brightest or something. I'll work tomorrow, but I always make sure to be home well before then. Except that this time, I'll be coming here."

"It sure is a hell of a way to celebrate your birthday. This is a big one, too."

She nodded as she thought about what he said about the planets aligning. She knew he wasn't serious when he said it, but it was very serious to her. She didn't know if astronomy played any part of it, but she knew that turning thirty on Friday the thirteenth during a full moon was very significant. Since she had been through so many full moons, Nada knew that the cycles rotated from twenty-nine to thirty days. The fact that this one hit after thirty days was definitely significant. So many threes. She wondered if thirteen would show up again. That thought stayed with her, as the chills returned.

# Chapter Fifteen

The next day Nada made sure she left work on time. She stood at her locker, when Mia stopped her.

"Hey girl, you want to hang with us tonight?" She asked.

"I'm sorry, Mia, I have an appointment that I can't break."

Mia looked at her watch and raised her eyebrows. "Who makes *appointments* after 9:00 on a Friday night?" She placed her hands on her hips. "I tell you, girl, if you keep turning me down, I'm going to start thinking you're avoiding me."

Nada pulled her purse out of her locker before closing it. "Oh, it's not that. I really do have to be somewhere. Maybe we can do something next weekend?" She offered.

"I'll hold you to that. The four of us can double: you and Dr. Zack, and me and my little man."

"Oh, Mia, you are such a matchmaker." Nada smiled upon hearing the nickname Mia had given her boyfriend, Jamal. "I'll see you Sunday."

"OK, girl. You have fun on your *appointment*."

Nada knew that wasn't possible, but she smiled her thanks.

When she got to Grady's clinic, Nada let herself in. She locked the door behind her and headed for his office. He wasn't there, so she walked to the lab. She found Grady standing beside the cage.

"Hi," she announced to his back. "What ya doin'?"

He looked over his shoulder at her. "Just testing the cage. Since we don't know what's going to happen, it's better to be safe than sorry."

She nodded. "Speaking of which, it would be a good idea to lock the cage this time." The cage only had a latch. There was a chain wrapped around one of the bars, with a combination lock attached. Grady never used it while she was inside.

He looked at her for a moment before stepping aside. She immediately noticed the new lock on the door. She stepped forward to get a better look.

"That's what I did today." He explained as she tugged on the door. "It's reinforced steel, like the cage." As he continued, his guilt was obvious in his tone.

Nada jerked on the door one more time before turning to him with a smile. It faded slightly when she noticed his expression, and she placed a hand on his arm. "It *is* better to be safe than sorry. I'm glad you thought ahead. I'll feel better about *changing* now."

Grady looked at the clock, and Nada followed his gaze. It was just after 9:30. He wrung his hands as he looked back at her. "Do you want to get inside now?"

Nada shook her head. "I'll have plenty of warning."

Grady looked at her face closely. "Did work go well?"

"Yeah, Mia got me a cake and everyone sang." She replied and rolled her eyes.

"Oh, that's right. Happy Birthday!" Grady exclaimed and headed for his office. He returned with his hands behind his back.

Nada fought the smile. Had he actually gotten her something?

Grady first revealed his left hand, which held a single red rose. She took it from him and smelled it. He then gave her a wrapped package. She nearly tore off the paper and let out a squeal. It was a coffee mug with a miniature version of the poster she crumpled and threw away. Her favorite vampire smiled up at her. "Oh, my God!" She impulsively hugged him. "Thank you!"

She pulled back to admire the mug. It touched her that he remembered her mentioning the show. "I love it." She placed it on the counter and put the rose inside.

"I'm glad. It was either the mug or a Martini glass, and I know you don't like liquor."

Nada placed her purse next to the mug. She looked at him and smiled warmly as tears formed in her eyes. As far as she could remember, she never had anyone in her life that cared enough to know what she did or didn't like. She kissed the fingertips on her right hand and then placed her fingers to his cheek. "It's great."

Nada stepped out of her shoes and pushed them next to the counter. She looked at Grady, who had both hands stuffed into the front pockets of his pants. "Is it OK to admit I'm a little nervous?" She asked him, knowing that he was very nervous. She could smell his fear. When she realized she *could* actually smell it, she looked back at the clock. It was ten 'til.

"Yeah, I think so," he replied before noticing her flushed face. He then followed her gaze to the clock. "Is it time?"

She nodded and headed for the cage. She stopped at the threshold and began to undress. "I don't want to leave my clothes inside."

Grady averted his eyes as she stripped. When he heard the cage door click shut, he walked over to it. Nada sat in the chair and leaned forward. Her long hair fell over her shoulders, protecting her modesty. Grady locked the door and pulled out the key. He then unlocked the combination lock and ran the chain around the two bars. After making sure it was secure, he reattached the lock and snapped it closed. He then picked up her clothes, stepped back and kept his eyes on Nada.

She began to rock back and forth on the chair. Her body heated up, and she wished she had water to splash on her face. Knowing that it wouldn't last long, she didn't bother to ask Grady. Nada looked up at him and decided to keep her gaze on him for as long as she could. She could only hope he would still be there when she awoke later.

Grady kept looking from Nada to the clock. A few minutes past 10:00, Nada stood and began to pace. Sweat glistened on her pale skin, and Grady couldn't look away from her nakedness. It was then that her scent reached him. His eyes widened sharply as he felt his erection. He sucked in his breath.

"Oh my, God!" He groaned and leaned forward slightly, his breath quickening. He took the cage's key out of his pocket and threw it on top of the cabinets. Since they stood several feet above his height, he would need a stool to retrieve the key later. Grady looked back at Nada, who paid him no attention. He looked back to where he threw the key. He tried to identify where the impulse came from to throw it up there. As Nada's scent grew stronger, he groaned and doubled over. There was no way his heated brain could puzzle that one out.

Nada mumbled something incoherent as she circled the cage. Grady hoped she *changed* soon, and he hoped her scent *changed* with her. He dropped to his knees, and his palms landed on the floor. He crawled over to the operating table and pulled out a drawer on the cabinet next to it. He scrounged through it until he found the package of masks. Extracting one, he quickly put it over his nose and mouth. He took a deep breath. He could still smell it, but it wasn't as strong. He sat on the floor and looked back at the cage.

Nada crouched on the floor. She arched her back and stretched her arms out in front of her. This time Grady didn't want to watch her *morph*, but he couldn't tear his eyes away from her damp skin. He decided he must have thrown the key out of his reach so that he wouldn't be tempted to join her in that cage. Grady pressed a hand over the mask, and slammed his other fist against the cabinet. His erection was painfully hard, and he didn't think he could bear much more. "*Change*, damn you!" He yelled at her. His eyes widened as she let out a low growl. Her eyes finally locked on him as she began to *change*.

"Oh no!" He mumbled, as he became aware of what animal she was becoming. A few minutes later, the black panther began to circle the cage. She'd stop every few minutes and look around. Grady cringed as she let out a loud rasping growl, which he felt confident was her mating call.

Grady let at least fifteen minutes pass before taking off the mask. He managed to get himself under control during that time, so he stood and sniffed the air before taking a deep breath. He sighed, as he was reassured that he wouldn't be affected by her scent as a panther. When he told Nada what happened, he'd leave that part out. He chuckled in embarrassment, glad that she hadn't been aware of what she did to him.

He tossed the mask on the counter next to the sink and splashed cold water on his face. He then headed for the fridge. After pouring some blood into a bowl and warming it up, he walked over to the cage. He bit his lip as he wondered how he should give it to her. If she had no control over the panther, he didn't want to get too close. He put the bowl down about two feet from the cage and looked around the lab. When he spotted a broom in the corner, he walked over to it. Bringing the broom back with him, he used it to push the bowl under the groove in the cage door.

Nada threw herself against the bars at him, and he jumped back so fast that he fell. He sat there and stared at her. She hissed at him and backhanded the bowl. It slid back under the door and right past Grady. It hit the cabinet on the other side of the lab and blood splattered everywhere.

He decided to end the experiment right there. He wasn't going to give her a live animal to abuse. She obviously didn't want to be messed with and would most likely kill anything put in front of her. Grady stood and went for the mop. He didn't want the blood to dry on anything.

He had everything cleaned up by 10:45. Nada let out another mating call while he cleaned. It made the hair on the back of his neck stand on end. Grady couldn't wait for the night to end.

At midnight he decided to get some paperwork done. While he worked on it, he wondered how he would stay awake all night. It was strange how that never occurred to him before. If he was to monitor everything that happened to Nada, he had to stay up until she *changed* back.

Grady rubbed his eyes and tried to concentrate on the paperwork in front of him. He poured himself another cup of hot coffee and drank it black.

It was almost three in the morning, when he heard the glass break. He had nodded off, and the noise made him nearly fall out of his chair. Fearing that Nada had somehow gotten out of the cage, he raced to the lab.

He ran into the room but froze when he saw her. She stood motionless and rigid in the cage, and she stared at something. Grady turned to look and saw that the back window was shattered. Glass and bloody prints were all over the floor. Even from across the room, Grady could tell they weren't human. He slowly eased across the room, staying close to the wall. He had just pulled a drawer open and reached in, when he heard the roar. The breath knocked out of him as he was attacked from behind.

The weight of the huge black panther far exceeded Grady's. He crumpled under the impact and landed hard. As he was mauled, he tried to drag himself out from under the huge beast. His fingers tried to grab hold of anything, and he noticed the broken glass. He screamed as he felt claws ripping into his back and reached for a piece of the glass. He turned as best he could. The panther was ready to rip his throat out, when Grady stuck the shard into its chest. It let out a surprised yelp and bolted across the room. In one jump, it landed on top of the cage. Grady turned over and groaned. The panther scratched him all the way down his back. He looked at the cage and watched Nada leap on top of the chair and try to climb the bars. She reached one black paw up as high as she could. The male let one of his own paws drop down between the upper bars, and their claws scraped against each other.

Grady could only shake his head in shock. The male was almost twice the size of Nada. The manther had trouble getting over being stabbed, and it growled at Grady. He wished he could growl back. That bastard nearly killed him.

At first Grady thought his eyes were playing tricks, but then he realized the manther was *changing*. In a few minutes a naked man with black hair jumped down from the cage. He slammed the combination lock against the bars, and it broke off in his hand. He then tested the strength of the door lock before glaring at Grady. "Give me the key, human." Kyros snarled.

"I don't have it." Grady replied before dropping his gaze to the man's bare chest. Kyros had Nada's regenerative abilities, and the wound he inflicted already healed. Grady wished he had the same healing ability. He felt light headed from his own wounds. He fell over onto his stomach and closed his eyes. He wondered if he was bleeding to death.

Kyros walked over to Grady and kneeled down. He went through all his pockets. When he couldn't find the key, he looked through every drawer and then tore apart Grady's office looking for it.

Grady lifted his head and saw the contents of several drawers in front of him. His gaze stopped on the object he had been searching for when he the panther attacked. Grady looked toward his office before reaching for it.

Kyros was in a rage as he left Grady's office. He headed for the cage, intending to break open the door. Nada yowled as he drew nearer. He began yanking on the door, not even noticing Grady as he pushed himself to his feet.

Grady's vision blurred as he stood. He closed his eyes for a moment and took a few deep breaths. He'd only have one chance. If he failed, he would most likely die. He opened his eyes and watched Kyros. He looked strong enough to break that lock if he kept pulling on it. Grady pushed himself away from the cabinet and moved closer to Kyros.

Nada let Kyros know about Grady by rearing up on her back legs and letting out a roar. It saved Grady by surprising Kyros, and he actually stepped back. That put him even closer to Grady. Kyros turned around swinging, but Grady was ready and brought the stunner up to land just under Kyros' armpit. Grady wasn't able to avoid the punch, however; and it threw back across the room. He landed on his wounded back; sheer will enabling him to keep hold of the stun gun. The pain was too much to bear, but he rolled onto his side, fighting to stay conscious.

Kyros stumbled back and fell against the cage. The stun should have knocked him out, but he fought against it. "You will die for this," he yelled to Grady. He dropped his gaze to the stun gun and snarled, exposing his sharp white teeth. His strength gave out, and he fell to his knees. Kyros took a deep breath and shook his head, "but not tonight." He looked back at Nada, who nuzzled his back. He reached through the bars and scratched under her chin.

Grady's eyes widened as he heard her purr. "Soon, my love." Kyros told her, before looking back at Grady. "You won't always have a weapon and don't think you can count on her to save you the next time we meet." Kyros gestured to Nada as he leaned forward to place his palms on the floor. He never broke eye contact with Grady. "She belongs to me, and she'll stand by and watch as I kill you." His breath grew shaky, and Grady was relieved to see the stun finally taking effect. Grady forced himself to sit up and held the gun higher.

Kyros hissed at him and then *morphed* back into the panther. He spared Grady one last glance before jumping through the broken window. Grady's eyes flew back to Nada as she let out a piercing wail, and then all was black.

## Chapter Sixteen

When Grady came to, the first thing he noticed was the pillow beneath his head. He tried to focus on it to make sure that's what it really was. He then noticed he lay in a bed. Since he lay on his side, he rolled onto his back to look around the room. He regretted the move instantly, as pain shot through him. He forgot about the scratches. He sat up and looked around the hospital room. How did he get there?

Shock rendered him speechless as Nada pushed open the door and walked in. She gasped when she saw him awake, and ran to his side.

"Are you OK?" She asked quickly and placed a hand to his face.

He reached up and grabbed her hand. Was he dreaming? He looked into her eyes, which filled with tears. "What happened? How did you get out of the cage?"

She took a step back at his question. She temporarily forgot that as she worried about him. When she *changed* back, it was just before dawn. She noticed the broken window first, and then she saw Grady. There was blood everywhere, and she thought he was dead. She kicked the door without even thinking, and it opened. After checking to see if he lived, she called the ambulance.

"It wasn't very hard," she replied. She feared asking him what happened. "Was it Kyros?"

Grady let go of her hand. Everything came back to him. "Was it like every other full moon? You don't remember anything?"

She shook her head and wiped her eyes. "Did I turn into a panther?"

"Yes, and it was Kyros. He's just like you."

"He was a panther?" She asked, and her voice grew shaky.

"At first, and then he turned into a man." If Nada had been able to open the cage, Kyros' next pull would've opened that door. Grady stunned him just in time.

"What did he look like?" She asked.

He shrugged and then regretted it. He groaned lightly at the pain in his back. "He's about my height, with short black hair. He's pale like you, and very muscular. I didn't get a good look at his face, but I wouldn't be any good at describing it even if I had." He looked toward the window, but the drapes were drawn. "What time is it? How long have I been here?"

Nada looked at her watch. "It's a little after two in the afternoon. You've been here since dawn." She wrung her hands, and Grady finally noticed she was nervous. He could only imagine how curious she was about what happened, but she obviously feared asking.

"How are you feeling?" He finally asked her.

She blushed and looked away. "Not like I usually do after a full moon."

Grady's eyes widened slightly. He had been afraid of that. "What do you mean?"

She shrugged and swallowed hard. "Well, I'm still on my period. It's always been gone the day after the full moon, but this time it isn't."

"Oh hell," he muttered. That left two options. Either she would have a normal heat, or she would remain in heat until she mated with Kyros. If it were the former, she would just have to avoid the manther until it was over. If it were the latter, Grady didn't know what to do. Would it be murder if he killed Kyros? The thought intrigued him, though it was more likely that since Kyros had come to town, Nada would only be in heat for a few weeks.

His gaze flew back to her worried face. If that were true, then Kyros would be coming for her that night. That also meant there could be a repeat performance of the night before. Grady knew he wouldn't survive another encounter with Kyros. The manther would be ready for him next time. Grady reached up and rubbed both hands over his face and temples.

"What is it?" Nada asked. She hated that he would make her ask what happened during the full moon. Judging by his reaction just then, there was plenty to say.

"Where's my doctor? I need to get out of here." Grady replied and shoved the covers back.

While Grady dressed, Nada left the room in search of his doctor. She walked past the desk and waved to Mia.

"How is he?" She asked when Nada got closer.

"He's awake." Nada rounded the desk and came up beside her coworker. She reached for Grady's chart. Dr. Thorton admitted him through the ER but had transferred him to another doctor's care once he had a room. She found the name and turned to Mia. "Could you please page Dr. Ramirez?"

"Sure thing." She dialed the number, all the while looking at Nada. "Honey, are you OK?"

Nada nodded but didn't make eye contact.

"What happened last night, Nada?"

She finally made eye contact with Mia. "I don't know yet."

"Zack came by before he went home. He's worried about you. Said you didn't look like yourself when you came in with Mr. Duncan. He said you looked right through him, like he wasn't even there."

Nada barely remembered the chaos that occurred after calling for the ambulance. She feared Grady would die before they got to the hospital. She couldn't remember even taking her eyes off of him once they got there. She shook her head.

"I guess I'll have to apologize to him." She replied tonelessly. Nada looked toward Grady's room. He deserved the apology. She almost got him killed.

An hour later a dressed Grady got himself discharged. The doctor didn't want him to leave, but Grady promised to come back in if he relapses. The doctor worried that the animal that attacked him might be rabid, but Grady reassured him that it wasn't.

Nada didn't say another word until they were at the clinic. "I forgot to tell you that the police came with the ambulance. They wanted to know what happened, and I had to tell them that only you knew. They're going to want to talk to you."

Grady groaned and looked over at the car parked next to his. The driver's side door opened, and a man in a suit got out. "Here we go," he muttered and got out of the car.

Nada smiled at the detective as she got out of the car, but she didn't say anything. She walked over to the front door of the clinic and waited.

Grady walked to the front of his car and waited for the detective to reach him.

"Grady Duncan?" At Grady's nod, he continued, "I'm Detective Somerset. How are you feeling, sir?"

"Did the hospital tell you I was discharged or have you been sitting here all day?" Grady replied, ignoring the question. He was not in the mood for an interrogation.

"Well, sir, I haven't been sitting here all day." He replied. "I need to ask you a few questions about what happened in your clinic last night."

"Sure, would you like to come in?" Grady asked as he searched for the proper key. Nada followed the two men inside.

Grady walked straight to the lab, with both Somerset and Nada directly behind him. She stayed at the door, while the two men walked inside. Grady surveyed the damage, as Somerset whistled.

"Quite a mess you've got here. What did this, Dr. Duncan?"

Grady turned towards him and noticed Nada standing behind him. He then shifted his gaze to the cage. The door hung sideways on one hinge. Chills went down his back as he stared at it. He tried not to think about what would have happened had she gotten out as the panther.

"Well, I've been known to take in strays on occasion," Grady began. He hated to lie, but he was about to say a string of them. "Sometimes they're hurt, and other times they just need a home." Grady looked at Somerset, who pulled out a notepad and pen. "I fix up the hurt ones, or bathe the dirty ones, and then I find them homes. Well, this time, the stray was dangerous."

Somerset frowned. "What kind of animal was it?"

"At first I thought it was a big cat, but apparently it was a more aggressive breed than that." Grady fought wincing. He sounded incompetent, but at least he hadn't blatantly lied yet. To keep from making eye contact with the detective, he looked around the room. He dreaded cleaning up the mess.

It was almost as if Somerset could read his mind. "You're a vet and you didn't know the breed?"

Grady shook his head as he focused on something on the floor. He took a step forward and crouched down. A lone male eye stared back at him from a fragment of the broken mug he gave Nada for her birthday. Grady sighed. "I haven't been a vet that long, and there's only so much you can learn from books." He rolled his eyes, since he knew more breeds than most experienced vets did. Grady turned to face Somerset. "Why are the police involved in this, detective? No crime has been committed. I was attacked by an animal."

"Are you sure about that? Have you been threatened to stay silent to protect someone?"

"I don't think a human could leave those bloody paw prints or the scratches on my back, detective." Grady reminded him, as he let the fragment fall from his fingers. As the detective walked across the room, Grady's gaze locked with Nada's. She hadn't moved from the threshold, and he remembered when he met her. She looked like a deer caught in headlights. Her current expression was similar, and he wondered how she would react if it were her that the detective grilled with questions. Grady raised his eyebrows in a silent question, but Nada shrugged and looked away.

Somerset's sharp gaze went from the bloody prints to the cage door. He turned around in time to catch the silent exchange of the other two in the room, but he didn't comment on it. He looked from Nada to Grady. "I also don't think a *big cat* could tear a door off like that. Most of the damage was done from the outside. Did someone break in here to steal the animal? Could it have been a breed that was worth a lot of money? Do you know the man who stole it?"

"Nothing was stolen, detective. Only one animal did all this damage." Grady couldn't keep from stealing a look at Nada, who visibly flinched but recovered quickly. He swung his gaze around to the far wall. "It broke that window, it left those prints, it clawed my back, and it did the damage to that cage. There's nothing more to say." Grady replied, trying not to lose his cool, but the memory of the attack was too clear. He swung his gaze back to Somerset and glared at the man. He tried to stare down the detective but didn't feel very confident. Although Grady was taller, Somerset was much broader and most certainly outweighed him. By comparison the detective seemed the larger man.

At first Somerset didn't respond. He walked over to the window and looked outside. He then looked down at the bloody prints and broken glass.

"Are you saying the cat broke the glass during its escape?"

Grady looked at the glass on the floor. He was smart enough to know that the glass would be outside if that were what happened, but there wasn't anything else he could say. "Yes."

"Then how did these prints get here?" Somerset challenged.

Grady looked back at the floor and shook his head. If it wasn't one thing, it was another. He sighed softly. "Maybe it came back after I passed out." It was a damn good thing it hadn't, he told himself as he felt another chill. Without even meaning to, he glared at Nada, still feeling betrayed that she wouldn't have helped him. He immediately felt guilty by her hurt look, and he forced a smile.

Somerset smiled and knelt down. He folded a piece of paper from his notepad and scraped up some of the blood. Nada stepped forward, but Grady's look halted her. The detective stood and put the paper in a little zipper lock bag. He put everything into the inside pocket of his jacket.

"I'll run that blood so the record can show exactly what breed of cat it was. I guess that's all I can do. Unless you press charges against someone, or someone else presses charges against you, there's nothing left to investigate. I guess I've taken up enough of your time." He turned to leave but stopped when he reached Nada. He stared at the small woman who hadn't said a word the entire time he had been in the clinic. "You *are* the one who found Dr. Duncan, correct?"

She nodded and looked at Grady. "Yes, I was worried about him, and he wasn't at his apartment."

"Why were you worried about him?" Somerset asked, smiling.

"Uh, he stood me up for a date, and that's not like him." Nada looked back at Grady and smiled. "I looked for him all night."

Somerset pulled his notepad out again. He flipped a few pages. "And your name is Nada Berch?" She nodded. "What is your phone number and address, in case I need to ask anything? It's just procedure."

She gave him the information. He nodded and put the notepad away. "Thank you, ma'am." He looked back at Grady. "Thank you, Doc. I guess that's about it. Hope you feel better soon. Have a nice evening."

Neither of them moved until they heard his car pull away. Nada let out a strangled cry. "Oh, Grady, he took some of the blood!"

Grady didn't say anything at first, only stared down at the bloody prints.

"Grady!" She yelled, nearly hysterical.

"It isn't your blood, Nada, so calm down. I'd like to see if he has any better luck finding the breed." Maybe the police would hunt Kyros down and kill him. That thought actually brought a tight smile to his face.

"Grady, what are we going to do?" She asked, beginning to sob. She didn't think she could take much more of not knowing. She spent all day waiting for Grady to wake up, agonizing over what happened. If he didn't tell her soon, she felt she would go mad.

He finally looked at her. Guilt stabbed into him, and his hard look slowly softened. He went to her and put his arms around her. "I'm sorry, Nada. I can't imagine how it felt to wake up and find me, and then having to wait so long." He lifted his arm to look at his watch. It was almost 4:00. "We can't stay here."

He couldn't even be sure that Kyros wouldn't return before nightfall, though he felt certain that the only way he could find her was by her scent. That hadn't happened until she was about to *change*. As long as they stayed away from the clinic, Kyros wouldn't know where they were until then. "Let's go to my place, until we can figure out what to do next. I promise I'll tell you what happened last night once we're there."

Nada nodded and wiped her eyes. She took a few deep breaths and watched Grady walk around the clinic. Her gaze skimmed over the broken mug but stopped on the crumpled rose Grady also gave her. Nada leaned down to pick it up. She held it up to her nose and inhaled, trying to pretend last night never happened. She knew that was impossible and absently crumpled the stem in her hand, ignoring the pain as the thorns dug into her skin. She let the rose fall to the floor and watched as the small wounds in her palm healed. Nada put her fingers up to her mouth as she watched Grady gather up a few things. When he was done, they left.

As soon as they got into his apartment, Grady poured them both a glass of wine. Nada was too stressed out and needed to relax. He took the bottle with him when he walked into the living room. Remembering his cats, he walked into his bedroom. After making sure they were both in there, he closed his door. The greyhound was in the backyard as usual.

Nada looked up when he returned to the living room. She took a few sips of the wine. He didn't sit down but paced the floor in front of the coffee table.

"Are you sure you don't remember anything that happened last night?" He finally asked her.

She shook her head. "The last thing I remember is sitting in the cage and wishing I had some water." She paused a moment in thought. "There's nothing else until I woke up and found you."

Grady nodded, deep in thought. He was relieved she couldn't remember his strong sexual reaction to her. He winced as his groin tightened at the memory. "We're in trouble, Nada. At least I know I'm in trouble. Kyros told me that he plans on killing me for interfering last night, and I believe him. If I hadn't had this," he leaned forward and picked up the stun gun, "he would have killed me. Hell, he almost did."

Nada looked at the stunner. "You used that on him? What did it do?"

"It should have knocked him out, but at least it did hurt him. I could tell he wanted to finish me off, but he's not stupid.  One more blast of this, and he may have passed out.  I think he knew what I would do to him had that happened. I was practically leaning against the operating table. I'm just lucky he didn't know how close I was to passing out. Had he decided to come back last night, I don't think I'd be here today." Grady never had anyone look at him with death in his eyes before, and he didn't like it. Helping Nada was going to get him killed. As he looked at her, he tried to decide if she was worth that.

Nada licked her dry lips. "Maybe you shouldn't help me anymore. I don't think I could live with myself if Kyros killed you."

"You didn't care last night." The words were out before Grady could stop them, and both he and Nada sucked in their breaths at the same time.  He groaned and she gasped.

"What happened, damn it?" She finally demanded.

Grady looked into her eyes and sighed. "If you hadn't been in that cage last night, I'm pretty sure you would have helped him kill me. You've only killed animals before, Nada, but I think it's different this time. Since Kyros is here, he must know that the countdown is over. Whatever this *thing* is inside you, it wanted him in whatever shape he was in.  Whether he was the panther or the man, you couldn't get close enough to him. You even warned him that I was about to shock him. Luckily, it didn't prevent it, or who knows what would have happened. I was odd man out last night, and it scares the hell out of me."

Nada was speechless. She had been afraid that she would want Kyros, but it horrified her that Grady felt she might actually kill *him*. Kyros was the one she wanted to kill, not Grady. "I need to remember what he did to me."

Grady nodded. "I agree, but how?"

She clicked her thumbnail against her top front teeth in thought. "How do you think he found me last night?"

"He followed your scent." He replied quietly.

Nada frowned at the response. "Does the male always find the female, or can the female find the male?"

"What do you mean? You need to avoid him, not find him." Grady responded.

Nada shook her head. "No, I mean what if I found him before I *change*?"

"What good would that do? You wouldn't know how you'd react around him until it was too late."

"Full moon is the only time I don't have control when I *change*." She insisted.

Grady shook his head in frustration. "That was before last night. I think the rules have changed."

"How do you know that?" Nada asked, curious about what he held back from her.

"You weren't there last night…Uh, I mean the Nada I know wasn't there. Everything was different. When you changed into the panther weeks ago, you were different. There was strangeness in your eyes last night. Maybe it was just because you were in heat, but maybe it was because Kyros has control over you. He told me last night that I wouldn't be able to count on you to help me, and I believe him. I think he's stronger than us both." Grady tried to swallow the lump in his throat.

He looked across the room and noticed the light on his phone blinked. Grady walked over to it and read the display. He had three new phone calls. There weren't any messages on his answering machine, so he scrolled through the caller ID. The three phone calls came from the same place. The name of a motel was listed above the number. He scrolled through again, noting the times. One was early that morning, and the remaining two were spaced out just a few hours earlier. Who would be calling him from a motel?

"What is it?" Nada asked from across the room.

"Probably nothing," but Grady jumped when the phone rang. Turning to look, he wasn't surprised to see the same motel calling. He hesitantly picked up the handset. "Hello?"

"Is this Grady Duncan?" The voice asked. Grady got a chill as he recognized it.

"Yes, Kyros." He saw Nada flinch as he said the name.

"I never told you to call me that." Kyros nearly snarled.

"Are you actually staying in a motel? I would think you'd be sleeping in the trees." Grady couldn't help but goad him, even though he knew it wasn't a smart thing to do. He looked at the phone number on the Caller ID and tried to remember where that prefix was in the city. He'd look it up after the call ended, but he was pretty sure it was downtown.

"Is she with you?" Kyros asked, ignoring the remark.

"Who?" Grady faked innocence, and he heard a loud sigh.

"I have your phone number, so it would follow that I know where you live. Or should I say where you *lived*?"

Grady closed his eyes at the not so subtle threat. Now he wished they were vampires, then Kyros couldn't come into his home without being invited.

"I'll keep her away from you." Grady told him with conviction he didn't feel. He was surprised when Kyros laughed.

"Why do you want to die? Stop interfering, since you're just wasting what little time you have left. Just because I can't smell her now, does not mean I won't find her. All I have to do is get close enough to her. She'll do the rest all on her own."

Grady opened his mouth to speak, but he hadn't realized that Nada walked up behind him. She grabbed the phone from his hand and yelled into the handset.

"What do you want with me?"

"It is so nice to hear your voice, my love." He said after a long pause. Nada thought he hung up, but the endearment made her cringe.

"You missed your chance last night. Why don't you just leave? I don't want you." She told him.

"Yes, you do. You just don't know it yet. Don't worry about last night, my love. We have twelve more chances, but I'll only need one of them." He practically purred.

Twelve more chances? Nada groaned as she realized what he meant. She knew thirteen would show up somewhere. That was what changed. Instead of her heat just lasting until the full moon was over, Kyros had thirteen days to mate with her before her heat would end. "Oh, hell...what happens if you miss all your chances?" She asked him. Grady mouthed *what*, but she shook her head and held up a hand.

"That won't happen, so why even discuss it?" Kyros teased her.

"What would happen?" She demanded.

"Then I go away and come back in three years. See, you need me. There is so much you need to learn from me.  Once we mate, all will become clear. Haven't you felt lost these last few years? Haven't you felt that a part of you was missing? Come to me." He pleaded.

Nada wondered why he asked her to go to him. Why didn't he just come to her? "Will tonight be a repeat of last night? I mean will it be just like full moon?"

Kyros didn't answer right away, and Nada feared that he wouldn't.  "You've not learned control yet?" He asked, and Nada could pick up the disappointment in his tone.

"You know about that?" She asked in surprise. What else did he know?  Was it true that he controlled her?

"I know everything about you, my love, though you should have mastered control by now. Don't worry, I'll help you. You've just been fighting your true nature. Give in to it, and everything else will fall into place. Come to me." This time he demanded.

"No!" She replied and hung up the phone. Her hand still rested on the handset, when it rang again.  She jumped back with a shriek.

Grady stepped forward and grabbed it without checking the Caller ID.

"Leave her alone, asshole!" He yelled.

"Excuse me?" A different voice responded.

Grady winced and looked at the display.  It only listed the city over a different number, so he assumed it was a cellular phone.

"I'm sorry.  I thought you were someone else."

"Crank calls?"

"Yeah, who is this?" Grady finally asked.

"Detective Somerset.  I'm calling from the lab. I had them do a rush on that blood.  I'm afraid I won't be able to close this case yet.  Human DNA was found in the sample.    We're crosschecking it with yours before we decide if criminal charges need to be filed.   Oh, and by the way, you had a breed of leopard in that cage. I'd like to know how a trained vet could mistake that for a cat."

## Chapter Seventeen

Grady closed his eyes and had to stifle the groan. How could he have forgotten that human DNA would be in that blood cocktail? He wondered how many different species of animal were in Kyros' blood. "Well, both the leopard and cat are felines. Was there anything else in the blood sample?"

"Good try at changing the subject, Dr. Duncan. Are you really a vet? Maybe I should verify your credentials."

"Mistaking a panther for a cat is not breaking the law, detective." Grady didn't know what would happen when they verified that the DNA wasn't his. Would they think he killed someone? Besides the blood, they didn't have a body. If he killed Kyros as a panther, would he stay that way or change back to a human?

"I didn't say the leopard was a panther. How did you know that?" Somerset asked smoothly.

Grady's eyes widened, and he clenched his teeth. He had fallen right into that trap. Luckily, his mind worked fast. "Since the leopard was completely black, it had to be a panther."

"Is that right? Learn something new every day. Well, there was only one other blood type in the sample, but it hasn't been identified yet." Somerset said, finally answering Grady's earlier question.

"Besides those three elements, did they find anything strange about the blood itself?" Grady asked, even though his thoughts remained on the fact there were only three types of DNA. Kenny had found so many types in Nada's blood, that he couldn't name them all.

"The technician is still working on it, but he thinks the sample was contaminated. I don't know anything about blood. Why are you so curious about it?" He asked suspiciously.

"I'm interested in everything about animals."

"If you say so, Doc. I mainly called to tell you not to leave town. When we get our facts straight about this blood, I'll be in touch."

"I'll look forward to that." Grady replied and hung up. He turned to face Nada, who chewed on her cuticles. He smiled and pulled her hand out of her mouth. "We've got to get out of here. We need to go somewhere that isn't connected to either of us."

Once they were in his car, Grady asked Nada about her conversation with Kyros. She relayed as much as she could remember.

"So you have to avoid him for twelve more days?" He groaned and leaned his head against the back of his seat. He never before felt so exhausted. He didn't know where to go, so he just drove.

Nada looked off in the distance. The sun already dipped below the treetops. "Oh, I wish the sun didn't have to set." She moaned softly.

Grady looked toward the sunset. As his gaze moved back to the street in front of him, something clicked in his mind. He thought about the last thing Kyros told him before Nada pulled the phone from his grasp. Kyros said that he couldn't *smell* her, but that all he needed to do was get close enough to her.

"When you asked Kyros if tonight would be just like full moon, what did he say?" Grady asked her.

Nada thought about it for a moment and then shook her head. "He didn't really answer, but he asked me to go to him twice. That struck me as odd. Why doesn't he just come to me? That's what he did last night."

Grady nodded and for the first time felt hope. "I don't think he can find you. I have a feeling that last night was the only time you couldn't control *changing*, since it was full moon. That night started this thirteen-day cycle, but I'm beginning to think that until it ends, Kyros has to be near you to set it off. That's why he wants you to go to him."

Nada's brow furrowed in thought. "So there's a chance I'll be OK tonight as long as I stay away from him?"

At his nod, she smiled. It had been awhile since Grady saw her smile, so he was glad to be able to give her a bit of good news. He could only hope he was right.

Grady realized he entered the downtown area, but he hadn't actually planned to drive there. While Nada talked to Kyros, Grady looked up the prefix of the motel's phone number. There was only one of that particular motel in downtown, and Grady knew its location. He was currently one block away. He looked at Nada and bit his lower lip. How close did she have to be to Kyros? Grady stopped the car one block away from the motel and parked on the side of the street.

"That is where Kyros called from," he said as he pointed to the motel.

Nada followed his gaze but then looked at the area surrounding the motel. "Grady, look what's behind it."

Grady did look and could only blink at first. One of the city's largest parks was downtown. They currently parked on the street that passed in front of it. Grady's gaze moved up the street until it stopped on the entrance of the park.  It stood directly across the street from his car.

Nada suddenly felt warm. She felt her forehead, and the moisture surprised her.  She hadn't been sweating until right then. She took a deep breath and turned to Grady. He looked at her flushed face and gasped.

"What is it?" Instinctively, he reached up and plugged his nose, and began breathing through his mouth. He looked toward the setting sun, which set enough to turn the sky orange. He then looked back at Nada, who arched her back and hung her head over the back of the seat. Grady saw movement and looked at the entrance of the park to see Kyros running toward them.

"Oh hell!" Grady yelled as he put the car in gear and slammed on the accelerator. Kyros jumped over the car parked in front of him and raced down the street behind them. Luckily, there weren't that many cars on the road just then, so Grady had a clean shot to the freeway onramp.  Kyros kept up at first but fell behind when Grady pulled onto the freeway and leveled his speed at 80 mph. When he could breathe easier, Grady turned to Nada. "You OK?"

Nada slowly opened her eyes and looked at her arms.  She wasn't *changing*. She turned to him with accusing eyes, too irritated with him to be relieved that he had been right. "Please tell me that experiment wasn't planned."

Grady shook his head as he looked in the rear view mirror.  The panther was nowhere to be seen, and he slowed the car to 70.  He lowered his window and then sniffed the air.  Thankful he didn't smell anything, he took in a breath through his nose. "It wasn't an experiment. I had no idea he was in the park."

"Even though you knew he liked trees?" She commented.

"Panthers like trees," he responded but that gave him pause. Kyros *had* been a panther when he chased the car, and the sun hadn't completely set. Grady looked at Nada. She stayed in her true form most of the time. She only *morphed* to feed or when she had no control over it. Was the panther Kyros' animal of choice, or was that *his* true form? He remembered Nada's question about why Kyros didn't have a real name. Animals didn't have names unless humans gave them one. Kyros thought he owned Nada, which would explain why he chose his name the way he had.

Things started clicking in his mind so quickly, that Grady had trouble keeping up. Nada could turn into any animal she fed upon, which was why she had all their DNA's in her blood. Kyros only had three DNA's in his blood: human, panther and the uncharted one. Grady could immediately rule out that Kyros didn't have time to kill as many animals as Nada had, since he was the one who infected her almost three years ago. Grady could also rule out Kyros being a purebreed of the uncharted DNA, since he had the other DNA mixed in. If he had been infected as a panther, that meant he only fed on humans. Grady gasped as he tried to comprehend what kind of human he could be when he started out as a vicious killer of an animal. "Why did he have to be a panther?"

"What?" Nada asked, wondering where that question came from.

At first Grady hadn't been aware that he spoke aloud. He looked at her and shrugged. "Panthers are the most vicious of all leopards. Too much melanin makes their coat completely black as opposed to just the normal black spots that leopards have. Since it's different, the panther's mother isolates it from the rest of her cubs. That leads to a more aggressive animal." Grady explained.

"What are you saying?" She asked, completely confused.

"I'm saying that you were human when Kyros infected you, but I think he was a panther when something infected him."

# Chapter Eighteen

Grady drove to the north side of town, which was as far away from downtown as he could get and still be in the city. He drove to a restaurant, since he realized he hadn't eaten all day. Once seated at the table and meals ordered, Grady looked out the window.

Nada took advantage of his distraction to study him. She lucked out meeting someone who knew so much about animals, but would that even matter if they encountered Kyros again? She wished her memory would come back. Not knowing what was coming was nearly unbearable. Before meeting Grady, she managed to live and work with little complication. Of course, she never trusted anyone and didn't really have a life. Nada suddenly realized that Kyros would have shown up with our without Grady. How would she have handled all this without him? Thinking along those lines, how was she supposed to continue her life the way it had been?

"I have to work tomorrow night." She said suddenly.

Grady turned from the window and looked at her. "Call in sick."

She nodded and looked at the tables close by. When she decided no one was within earshot, she leaned forward. "I'm going to need some blood soon, and I only have enough for today and tomorrow. I was planning to get more at work, but if I can't get to my apartment..." She faded out without finishing.

"When was the last time you fed?" Grady thought to ask.

She could do nothing but stare for a few minutes. When she woke that morning and found him covered in blood, she felt her teeth sharpen. That was the second time it happened in less than a month, and it worried her. "While I was waiting for the ambulance, I drank some from your fridge." She cringed, still remembering how bad it tasted cold.

"That's good," he replied, noticing how long it took for her to answer. "So you should be OK until tomorrow?"

She nodded and then shrugged. "Yeah, I feel alright for now." She just wanted the day to be over and wanted to sleep away the next eleven.

Grady looked at the other tables also. There still wasn't anyone seated nearby. "If Kyros isn't human, we do have an advantage over him."

"How's that?" She asked, again thankful he knew so much about animals.

"He can't be educated. Without knowing how the system works, he couldn't even get a fake social security card. He can't have credit, so he can't rent a car let alone own one. He probably came into the country as an animal and snuck onto a ship or something. Since he can't carry clothes around when he's a panther, he won't run around the city as a man. That means he has to wait until dark before venturing out." He paused as he remembered the phone call. "Unfortunately, he was smart enough to figure out who I was and how to find my phone number. That means he knows how to read, since he most likely found my name at the clinic. How would he know how to read?" He said the last question more to himself, but it got Nada thinking.

She shrugged. "Well, when I turn into an animal I've fed on, their personality strongly affects mine.  I instinctively know how to do everything they could do. We learn to read early, so maybe that knowledge becomes a part of us. If he's fed on a lot of humans, each one may make him smarter." She shrugged again, since she felt she grasped at straws.

Grady thought about what she said. She definitely knew more than he did about what Kyros was capable of. "When you say personality, do you mean specific memories?"

Nada shook her head.  "No, nothing like that." Before she started volunteering at the hospital, she never fed upon human blood.  She had no interest in becoming a nurse back then. It hadn't been until after stealing a few pints of the donor blood, that she began thinking along those lines. She graduated ahead of schedule, since the courses had been easy enough to double up on her class load. It never occurred to her to wonder why they were so easy, but she graduated at the top of her class. It was entirely possible that doctors and nurses at the hospital donated blood that was stored there.  Had she acquired their knowledge? "Kyros may be more educated than you think he is," she finished.

Nada tried to think of what else she knew that hadn't always been there. She learned how to use a computer without being taught. She was able to change the oil in her car.  When she had a plumbing problem at her apartment, she had been able to fix it on her own. There were a lot of little things like that. None of it seemed obvious, until she stopped to think about it. To anyone else, it just meant she was an independent woman.  She looked at Grady and nodded.

"He may not even know it. There's nothing specific. He wouldn't know where to begin. If he knew enough to try something, he would stand a good chance of figuring it out. He's so wrapped up in trying to mate with me, that I just can't imagine he's calm or rational enough to think of it. Creating a human identity for himself may be just a bit out of his range, not to mention he would've had to feed on someone who knew how to do it. What are the odds on that happening? I think you're right about us having that advantage over him." She finished with a smile. Nada thought about her dreams. "He's been in my head, and I don't even think he knows my name. He kept calling me his *love*, but he never used my name."

They both looked up when the waitress came over with their food. As she laid the plate in front of Nada, the older woman smiled. "I hope you two don't plan on staying out too late tonight, not with a lunatic running around."

Both Grady and Nada looked at her sharply. "What lunatic?" Grady asked.

"Didn't you hear about the body that was found this morning? The neck was broken and the body drained of blood. God, will we ever be free of these lunatics?"

Nada closed her eyes. She always dreaded hearing of something like that right after a full moon, but this time she knew it wasn't her. So Kyros was a murderer. "That's awful." She told the waitress.

"You two be careful tonight. Well, enjoy your dinner." She told them and left.

Nada watched her walk away until she heard Grady's chuckle. She turned to look at him, unable to imagine what was funny. Grady noticed her look and shook his head.

"Now, don't look at me like that. I don't find Kyros' victim to be humorous. I just can't get over how our waitress tells us about such a gruesome death practically in the same breath as hoping we'll enjoy our dinner." He explained.

Nada nodded. "Yes, I've certainly lost my appetite."

"Well, try to eat something. I think we're both going to need to keep our strength up." Grady stretched his back slightly to test how it felt. It was still very tender, and he wondered if he had stitches. He didn't have the chance to look at the damage. Nada watched him and concern washed across her features.

"I'm sorry about what happened to you last night. How are you feeling?"

Grady shook his head. "You have nothing to be sorry about. You didn't twist my arm to help you, and there was no way for you to know how badly it would go." He drank some of his water. "I'll live," he finished.

Nada noticed how he wouldn't look in her eyes as he spoke. She pulled her lower lip between her teeth and gnawed on it. Even if it had been a full moon, how could she have wanted Kyros to hurt Grady? Did Kyros have such a strong hold on her? She looked back at Grady; thankful he was still willing to help her.

"If Kyros infected me and was infected as a panther, what was it that infected *him*?" She asked.

Grady stared for a moment. That question occurred to him, but he didn't want to voice it. Since she finally asked it, the answer could no longer be avoided. Unfortunately, only Kyros knew that answer. Grady shook his head.

"I don't know if we'll ever know that. Hell, Nada, you can't even remember Kyros, and he is the one who infected *you*."

She shrugged, not knowing what else to do. What would it take before her memories would come back? As she suddenly thought of the winged beast, she wondered if having them back would be a good thing.

After they ate, Grady drove them to a nearby motel. Their room had two full sized beds. Grady took one and Nada took the other. He collapsed on his immediately and groaned. "Just shoot me."

Nada smiled and walked to the sink. She got herself a glass of water and stared at her reflection as she drank it. She had the impulse to throw the glass at the mirror but managed to fight the need. Tears of frustration welled in the corners of her eyes, and she looked down. She sensed Grady approaching. He put his hands on her shoulders. She looked up and met his gaze in the mirror.

"I'm so sorry I got you into all this." She said, her voice shaky.

Grady turned her around so that she faced him. "Please stop apologizing. I'm just glad you had me to count on. We'll get through this, Nada. You just have to believe in that and have faith."

She looked up into his face. He wiped the tears away and then they embraced. She pressed her cheek to his chest and inhaled deeply. She let the air out of her lungs slowly, as she became aware of his heartbeat. It beat in time to hers. That seemed so intimate to her, as she tilted her head back to see his face.

Grady looked down for a moment before giving into instinct. Their lips met tenderly for their first kiss. It quickly became passionate, and Nada moved her fingers into the hair at the back of his head. It felt so right, even though she knew it was wrong. At that moment, she didn't care where it led. She just wanted to be close to him. She didn't have the faith to believe that everything would be OK, and this could be their last kiss as well as their first.

Grady pulled her body even closer and his hands moved down to cup her butt. He drew her up against his body, and she gasped as she felt his arousal against her stomach.

"No," she muttered and put her hands between them. She didn't have the strength right then to move any further away. She closed her eyes and waited. If Grady truly wanted her, she wouldn't stop him again.

"Got to save yourself for him, huh?" Grady said bitterly as he released her and stepped back.

"Don't say that." She pleaded, almost disappointed that he didn't try harder, but also relieved they wouldn't be making what she felt would be a mistake. "I don't want to hurt you, Grady. That is the last thing I would ever want."

Various scenarios went through her head at the prospect of them making love. What if she got too carried away and lost herself? She could turn into a dangerous animal and not even mean to. Who knew what she could do to Grady then?

He looked at her and took a deep breath. "I'm sorry I said that. I can't imagine how hard it is for you, but it isn't easy for me either, you know." He sat on the edge of his bed and leaned forward. "I'm just so tired." He finished and put his face in his hands.

"I know." She edged closer and moved her fingers through his hair. When he didn't pull away, she continued.

Grady closed his eyes and enjoyed her gentle caress. He had a vague memory of his mother doing the same thing when he was little. It always calmed him down. He wanted to wrap his arms around Nada and pull her onto the bed with him, but he didn't. He sighed deeply and without even realizing it happened, he drifted off.

Nada was surprised when Grady slumped over onto his side. She worried at first, until she heard his breathing. She smiled before reaching for him and pulling him to the head of the bed. She then took off his shoes and spread a blanket over him.

She sat on her bed and watched him for a while. Nada knew he should still be in the hospital and remembered how he looked that morning. He had been paler than she was, and the dark blood made a sharp contrast. She had a hard time swallowing the lump in her throat as she remembered how she felt when she thought he was dead. He had been lying in a pool of his own blood. Even though the sight of the red liquid caused her teeth to sharpen, she still approached him to feel for his heartbeat. Luckily, she didn't need to touch him to verify he lived. She heard his heart beating from several feet away. Her relief was short lived; however, as she looked down to see that she stood in his blood. She had to sprint to the fridge for the blood he kept there. She barely noticed its coldness and leaned against the counter's cool surface until her breathing regulated. Once verifying her teeth were back to normal, she reached for the phone and called an ambulance. Nada then walked back to Grady. Not minding the blood surrounding him, she kneeled next to him and touched his brow. It was at that moment that she realized how she felt about him. She still sat in the blood when the paramedics surrounded her.

What would Kyros do the next time they met? She cringed since she knew the answer. She shook her head in despair and pulled the covers back. It took her awhile before she fell into a fitful sleep.

She knew she dreamed. She stared off at the mountains for a moment and closed her eyes as the cool breeze caressed her face.

*Come to me, my love.*

Nada turned toward the voice, but she couldn't see him. "Where are you, Kyros?" She called.

*Look within yourself, and you'll know where I am. I'll be waiting for you.*

"I don't want to go to you. You're dangerous." She turned full circle, wondering why he wouldn't show himself.

*I'm only dangerous to those who stand between us, but never to you. You are my destiny, and I'm yours. Come to me, my love. It is the only way to save your friend.*

"What do you mean?" Nada asked, even though she knew what he meant.

*I will spare your male human friend, but only if you come to me now. If you make me find you, I will tear him apart piece by piece.*

Nada heard a growl behind her. She turned to see the black panther attack Grady. She gasped as his jaws closed around Grady's throat.

"Help me, Nada!" Grady screamed just before Kyros broke his neck. Nada reached out to him and screamed.

Nada sat up and choked on a scream. She clamped a hand over her mouth to keep it inside. She then turned to make sure Grady was all right. His breathing was steady as he slept on undisturbed. She pushed back the covers and moved over to his bed. Nada leaned over him and kissed him lightly on the cheek.

Grady slept late. When he finally awoke it was after ten o'clock in the morning. He yawned and stretched, before turning to look at the other bed. He wasn't immediately alarmed when he didn't see Nada. Her clothes were placed at the foot of her bed, and her shoes were on the floor. Grady got up and stretched again, thankful his back was healing. He walked over to the mirror and took off his shirt. He turned around and looked over his shoulder. He cringed when he saw the red gashes. They had been neatly stitched, but all four were almost a foot long. He shook his head and knocked on the bathroom door.

"Hey, you OK?" It was then that Grady saw the note. He had to read it twice before the words sank in.

> *Grady,*
> *I'm sorry, but I had to leave. Thanks for all your help, but I must do the rest on my own. Please forget about me. I love you.*
>
> *Nada*

"Oh hell!" Grady grabbed his car keys and ran from the room.

## Chapter Nineteen

As Detective Somerset waited for his coffee, his gaze lingered on the young girl at the register. Her hair and eyes were dark, and she reminded him of someone. He tapped his fingers on the counter top, as he thought about it. He always got his coffee at the café, but he'd never seen her before. She was obviously a new hire, so from where could he know her? Then it suddenly hit him. She looked like the woman at the vet's clinic. Somerset tried to remember her name. Hell, he was lucky to remember the vet's name. Duncan, yes that's what it was.

"Here you go, Cayle." His regular server handed him the coffee. He was ashamed to admit he couldn't even remember her name. His eyes dropped to her nametag, and then he smiled at the girl.

"Thanks, Deb. See you tomorrow." Cayle replied and walked out of the café. He needed to start working on name recognition. He usually related the name to the case, if he could. It didn't always work, but he hated to have to check the files all the time. He just dealt with way too many people. His workload had to be double that of any other detective in his precinct.

He thought about what relation he attributed to the girl's name. A tree came to mind, and then so did her name: Berch. Cayle would have to consult the file for her first name. He never bothered with learning those.

He walked past the front desk and headed for his office. The day would be a long one. He needed to remember to call the lab after lunch to find out if the human blood found at the vet's clinic was Duncan's or not. If it wasn't, then he might have a homicide on his hands. He'd hate to arrest the vet, but Cayle also knew the man kept something from him. He hated that more.

As he opened the door to his office, Cayle's thoughts returned to Miss Berch. There was something about her that intrigued him. He didn't know if he'd get the chance to find out what it was, but the coffee shop wasn't the only time someone else had reminded him of her. Her beauty wasn't what affected him so much. It was her eyes. They seemed more alert than most people's. There was something else, too, but he hadn't spent enough time with her to pinpoint it. He looked forward to their next meeting. As he wondered when that would be, he reached for the case file. He flipped it to the section where he wrote her information. He stared at her first name for a moment. Nada was an unusual name. In all the time he'd been a cop, he'd never before met a woman by that name. She was definitely unique. He pushed his chair back and stared out the window. He smiled as he wondered what she was doing right then.

# Chapter Twenty

Nada stared at the mountains and enjoyed the cool breeze. Hearing something behind her, she turned to look and found herself in a shipyard. She looked over her shoulder, but the mountains vanished, which came as no surprise. The mountains were always her first hint she was dreaming.

She heard the noise again and turned to see Kyros walking up a gangplank that led to a departing ship. His shiny black fur rippled with each step he took. She looked down at her arms, relieved to see her own pale skin. Nada looked back at the panther, which stopped halfway between the ground and the ship. Kyros turned to face her.

"Where are you going?" She thought to ask.

*There's no reason for me to stay any longer. I've been away from home long enough.* He replied inside her head. *When you're tired of this place, you'll know where to find me.*

She shook her head. "I don't know anything about you, Kyros. I'm glad you're leaving." Nada was very uncomfortable with how she felt. Why would he leave before he mated with her? As she felt the chills, she rubbed her hands up and down her arms. At least Grady would be safe once Kyros left.

Kyros looked at her for a moment. If it were possible for a panther to smile, that was exactly what he did.

*You only think you're glad. You are still so very young, my love. When you grow up, you'll realize we'll always be a part of each other.*

"Stop calling me that!" She yelled at him, wishing she could tear his voice from inside her head. "My name is Nada!"

*I will never acknowledge you by your human name. You are better than that, my love. I look forward to our next... encounter.*

Before she had the chance to think about that, he turned and leapt over the side of the ship and vanished from sight below deck. Nada fought the temptation to chase him down. There was so much she still needed to know. She bit her lip and turned to walk away.

Nada froze upon seeing the three men directly behind her. Her gaze went from Grady, to Detective Somerset and then to Doctor Zachary Thorton. Somerset and Zack moved closer to her. When Nada looked at Grady, he began to fade. She reached for him, but her hand went through him. He waved, and she shook her head.

"No!" She shouted with a gasp.

Shock kept Nada from screaming as she fell. She landed on the ground, causing leaves and dirt to fly about. She pulled a leaf out of her mouth as she turned to look up. A huge tree limb stretched out directly above her. Nada sat up and looked around. Through the darkness, she could clearly see the park around her. She leaned her head back against the trunk and stared at the limb. Had she actually been sleeping up there? Falling out of a tree wasn't exactly the best way to awake from a dream, especially the kind of dreams she'd been having lately. Looking toward the street, she saw the motel. It was then that she realized she sat in the park where Kyros emerged from as he chased Grady's car the night before.

Nada pushed herself up to a crouch and looked around again. "Kyros?" She called lightly. If he were close by, she wouldn't need to raise her voice. She suddenly realized she was naked in a public park. She didn't have a watch on, so she had no idea of the time.

She stood and pressed herself closer to the tree. Looking around the park, she made sure no one was around. Knowing that she couldn't stay there, she pictured a hawk. As soon as she *changed*, she flew home.

Nada landed on the windowsill of her apartment and pictured her human body. She looked through the window, and all was quiet. She pushed open the window and crawled in. Nada headed for her bedroom and pulled on a robe. As she passed the telephone, she noticed she had messages. She pushed play.

The first was from Grady. He sounded worried as he begged her to call and let him know where she was. Nada took a deep breath, unable to risk involving him until she knew that Kyros was gone. The next message was from Mia.

"Girl! Where the hell are you? You better be dead or close to it, to make me cover for you. You're just lucky I didn't have plans tonight. Call me!"

"Oh hell!" Nada groaned. She forgot to call in sick to work. She picked up the phone and called the hospital. She thought up a good excuse while she waited to be connected to her ward. Mia picked up the line.

"Mia, I'm so sorry. I was going to call in sick, but I guess I overmedicated and slept the whole day away. Thank you so much for covering for me. I owe you big time." She spoke quickly, trying to smooth over the potential explosion. Mia was a sweet woman, but she did have a temper when crossed.

"Damn right, you owe me, girl! By the way, Zack came by and asked about you. He's looking forward to next weekend."

"Next weekend?" She asked, as she thought about her dream. Why had Zack been in it? Then again, why had Somerset been in it? She shook her head.

"Don't tell me you forgot already? You said we could double." Mia reminded her.

"No, Mia, I didn't forget." Actually, she had, but she couldn't admit that. "I said that we would see."

"No, girl, we *are* going to double. Remember that you owe me now. I'm tired of you breaking Zack's heart. He's a sweetheart, and it's about time you realized that."

Nada felt a headache coming on and closed her eyes. She reached up and squeezed the bridge of her nose. She must not have fed all day. "Mia, I need to take some more medication and go to bed. Thanks again for covering for me. We'll talk more about doubling when I see you tomorrow."

"OK, you're off the hook for now. Feel better."

"Thanks, Mia, I will." She hung up and headed for the fridge, but her thoughts stayed on Somerset. There had to be some reason he was in her dream. Both he and Zack stepped closer to her as Grady faded away. That made no sense to her, but maybe it meant she could trust them. Knowing that Zack couldn't help with her current situation, she picked up the phone and called information. When Detective Somerset answered, he was very surprised to hear from her.

"Miss Berch, what can I do for you at such a late hour?"

Nada looked at the clock, surprised she hadn't been curious about the time before then. It was almost 10:00 at night. She was lucky that he worked late hours. "Well, Detective Somerset, I need help and thought you'd be the only one that could help me."

"Oh, and how's that?"

"I need to know if there is a shipyard or dock nearby, and if there are any ships scheduled to depart for Europe or Asia?" She asked and held her breath. What would he think of such a request?

He didn't respond right away, and Nada was forced to breathe. "Detective Somerset?"

"You may as well call me Cayle, Miss Berch." She heard him sigh. "There is a shipyard on the coast south of town, but I don't know about any ship schedules. I can call and find out if you'd like. Just give me the number where you'll be, and I'll call you right back."

"Uh, no, I won't be at any number for awhile. How long do you think it will take, and I'll call you back?" She stumbled through the lie, not even sure why she didn't want him to know where she was. He would assume she was at home. He could have caller ID for all she knew.

"It won't take long, Miss Berch. Try back in half an hour."

"Thanks, Cayle." She hung up and rubbed her temples. She should have fed before making the phone call to Somerset. Nada walked into the kitchen and opened the fridge. She grabbed the container and put it in the microwave. Not even giving it the full time it needed to heat up, she took it out and drank the blood down in a few swallows.

After rinsing out the cup and putting it in the dishwasher, she headed for her room. She dropped her robe in her clothes hamper and headed for the bathroom.

She never felt so dirty before and wished she could remember what she did all day.  She tried to focus on what she did after leaving Grady in the hotel room. As soon as she closed that door, she changed into a hawk and flew downtown. She remembered landing on a limb in one of the trees.  It could have been the same limb she fell off of, but she couldn't remember anything past that.

As Nada looked in the mirror, she shook her head. Was Kyros really leaving the country? She turned on the water and made sure it was good and hot.  As she lathered up her body, she suddenly realized her "heat" was over. There was no more blood and she was no longer swollen or tender.  "Oh hell!" She slammed her fist against the side of the shower, cracking the tile.  Since there was still over a week left before the thirteen days would be up, that could only mean one thing. She must have mated with Kyros earlier in the day.  She bit her lip and lifted her face, as tears filled her eyes. She let the hot water pour over her face and body, hoping it would clean away all traces of Kyros from her. Maybe she would wake up and find out everything had just been one long nightmare.

After Cayle hung up the phone, he stared at it for a moment.  The last person he expected to hear from was Nada Berch. For a reason he couldn't comprehend, he'd been unable to get her out of his head all day.

He was disappointed that the lab technician had left right after lunch and his assistant couldn't find the test results.  Cayle almost told the woman off, but he managed to hold his tongue.  He wished he worked such short hours.

He grumbled to himself as he turned to his computer.   He looked through his interoffice directory first and flipped a few pages trying to find the shipyard. Once he found it, he circled it with a pencil. His system was always online, so he typed in the URL of the shipyard. He would download the schedule, since he doubted anyone else would still be working. He looked at the clock; even more surprised that Nada called so late. Where was Doctor Duncan? That question echoed inside his head, so he looked up the vet's phone number and called him.

It was after 10:30 when Nada finally walked back into the living room, wearing a shorts set. She immediately noticed there was a new message on her machine, so she walked over and pushed play.

"Nada, are you there?" Grady paused for a moment. "Hell! Somerset just called me. He was too busy to talk, but he told me that you called about some ship to Europe? Is Kyros taking you with him? Damn it all to hell! Are you there?" Nada closed her eyes at his urgent tone. "Well, I have the address and I'm leaving now. I won't let you go, Nada. I love you, too, damn it!"

She winced as he slammed the phone down. She picked up her own phone and dialed his number, but it just rang. She then tried his cell phone, but all she got was a voice telling her that he was unavailable. Nada then dialed Somerset's number but only got his voice mail.

"Oh, hell!" She yelled at the four walls. She then called information and got the address and phone number of the nearest shipyard. She called but naturally no one answered at such a late hour. Getting frustrated, she grabbed her keys and headed out to her car.

# Chapter Twenty-One

As soon as Grady left the message on Nada's machine, he left his apartment. In his rush, he forgot to turn on his cell phone. He headed east on the freeway and hoped no cops were on the road, since he drove way above the speed limit. He was furious with Detective Somerset. How could the man call him and then not have the time to go into detail? Somerset told Grady to notify him as soon as he found out what was going on. When Grady asked him what Nada had said, Somerset replied that she asked about a ship going to Europe. The first thing the detective asked Grady was if he had been the one to have Nada call him. Grady didn't think Somerset believed him when he said he knew nothing about it. Somerset even made a comment about smuggling a dangerous animal across international waters. Grady knew that if a dangerous animal were going to Europe on a ship, it would be smuggling itself.

Grady didn't know what he would do when he confronted Kyros and Nada. Could he really stop her if she wanted to leave with the manther? Since Grady knew which dock to go to, he didn't have to waste time finding it. They were all clearly marked, and he parked in the appropriate lot. He opened his trunk and pulled out the flashlight and tire iron. He silently swore as he realized he forgot his stun gun. Grady took a deep breath as he closed the trunk.

He approached the dock slowly and kept to the shadows. It wasn't quite 11:00 and all was quiet. Grady turned his head as his ears picked up a sound. He couldn't figure out what caused it, but he followed it. He froze when he saw Kyros feeding on a dockworker. Grady swallowed the bile threatening to rise and turned away for a second. He shook his head and looked back. Since the panther was distracted, could Grady attack before being noticed? He held up the tire iron and moved closer.  Where was Nada?

He stood about ten feet away from the carnage, when Kyros moved away and began to *change*. As soon as he was a man, he turned to face Grady. His face and chest were covered in blood.

"Why did you come here?" Kyros asked. "Couldn't you leave well enough alone?  I am on my way home and was going to let you live.  Do you want to die?"

"I don't care where you go, but you aren't taking Nada with you.  Where is she?"

Kyros stopped to stare at him for a moment. Grady grew uncomfortable under his unnatural stare, since something was wrong with his eyes. The darkness masked the truth, but he didn't like it. Grady refused to look away as Kyros continued to stare.

"At home, I should think." Kyros finally said, but then stopped to think about it.  "No, she is in her car."

"You're lying," Grady responded, but the strange way the manther acted confused him. He turned to look back at the parking lot. Was she in her trunk? Of course, he hadn't noticed her car when he pulled up.  There was only one other in the lot, and Grady guessed it belonged to the dead worker.  Had Kyros put her in that car's trunk until he was ready to force her onto the ship? Then he remembered she had called Somerset about the ship schedules. Had Kyros forced her to make the call? If the full moon was any indication, she may not need to be forced to do anything. "Is Nada already on board?"

Kyros blinked and looked at Grady as if he were stupid. "I already told you that she is in her car. We finished our business hours ago, and I haven't seen her since."

"You already raped her?" Grady asked in shock.

Kyros scoffed at the question and looked astonished. "Rape? That is a human word."

"She *is* human, you bastard, which is more than I can say for you."

"She has not been human since the night I made her mine. We are better than that; better than you."

"Oh yeah? How do you spell Kyros?" Grady almost smiled at the manther's confused expression. "Did you pick that name yourself, or was it chosen by *your* master? What do you call *him*?"

Kyros tilted his head to the side and studied him. "I think I now know why she likes you. You are brave but not too bright." He looked at the tire iron in Grady's hand, undaunted by his hostility.

Grady tightened his grip on it and stepped to the left to move away. He also wanted to be able to see if anyone approached. Kyros turned to follow his movement, so that he faced away from the parking lot.

"Is that all you have this time? What do you expect to do with it?" Kyros asked, gesturing to the tire iron.

"I expect to crack your skull open with it." Grady replied, surprised by the surge of jealousy that coursed through him. They had most likely been panthers when the mating occurred, so there really was no reason for it. He tried to shake it off.

Kyros actually smiled and scoffed again at the idea. "That won't be enough. Just realize that as soon as I tire of talking to you and return to my true form, you will die quickly. I see no reason to prolong your death. I guess I owe her that at least."

"What, you can't kill me as you are? I guess you're not as strong as Nada is then. I know she could kick my ass in human form." Grady challenged, wondering why he insisted on goading such a dangerous creature.

Kyros' lips twitched, but then he forced a smile. "I see no need to fight you as a man, but I'm sure I would prevail in either case." He sniffed the air. "I wounded you the last time we met. You are still damaged, which would make it that much easier. You won't walk away from this battle. Even though I have just fed, I will gladly feed upon you before leaving on that ship."

Grady almost lowered his weapon. It finally sunk in that since he already mated with her, Kyros would leave without Nada. Panthers were solitary animals outside of mating season. Grady was puzzled. Why had Nada asked about ships to Europe if she hadn't been leaving with Kyros? His eyes widened slightly as he watched a car pull into the lot. It was too dark to recognize, and so was the figure approaching.

Nada drove around the shipyard, trying to find a ship that looked ready to leave. Ready to give up and try to find the office, she finally spotted Grady's car in one of the lots. She parked next to it and ran to the nearest ship. Nada could see the two men clearly and immediately recognized Grady. He brandished a tire iron at the tall naked man, who she figured had to be Kyros. He faced the other way, so she could only see his back. His white skin nearly glowed in the faint light from the dock. She ran faster. "Grady, get out of there!" She yelled.

Kyros turned to look over his shoulder, and Nada nearly tripped over her own feet. Only a couple yards separated them, and she couldn't take her eyes off of him.

"Derek?" She said the name without thinking. As she stared into the familiar face, the floodgate of memories began to crack open, and she dropped to her knees. She moaned and covered her eyes, trying to block out the onslaught. It had been three years since she last saw that face. Her 30th birthday marked the three years since he asked her to marry him. They backpacked across Europe together. They set up camp near a mountain lake in Germany, when he popped the question. She had been overjoyed, since she loved him for years. They met during her first year at college. Tears filled Nada's eyes as she began to remember all the wonderful times they shared.

Right then, she could only dwell on their final night together. Derek made a fire, and they made love beside it. She sat astride; her body full of him, when something attacked her from behind. It sunk its teeth into her shoulder. She tried to knock it away, but it hung on tight. Derek lay pinned beneath the combined weight of Nada and her attacker and couldn't move at first. They made eye contact, and she watched him reach for a log from the fire. She leaned to the side, and he struck the log against the creature.

It howled, pushed Nada aside and jumped over her to get to Derek. Nada then saw the panther. She never saw one up close before. In her weakened state she could only watch as it tore open Derek's throat. She cried out in anguish and buried her head in her arms.

When all was quiet, she lifted her head to look. Her mouth fell open, as she looked from what was left of Derek to the panther and watched as it *morphed* into Derek. She shook her head and tried to crawl away as he approached her on hands and knees. She looked from her dead fiancé to the creature that looked like him. Was she losing her mind? He reached out and grabbed her nearest ankle. He pulled her back toward him, and she held up her hands.

"No," was all she could say. Derek's blood covered him as he slid up her body, shoving her legs apart. As he entered her, she turned her head away and looked back at the bloody mess on the other side of the fire. Derek's eyes were open wide, but she knew he couldn't see. She opened her mouth to scream but nothing came out. She was barely aware of what the creature did to her, until he grabbed the hair at the back of her head. He then clamped his mouth on her wounded shoulder. She gasped as he began to suck the blood from her body. She tried to push him away but had little effect. When he finally lifted his head, she looked away from his bloody face; Derek's face. He scratched a fingernail across his upper chest and pressed her face to it.

"Drink," he demanded. She shook her head, and he shoved her face even closer. Feeling lighter headed by the minute from the blood loss; she knew she had no choice. She drank until he let go of her head. When he finished with her, she curled into a ball and cried.

As she remembered what he did to her, Nada felt a little of her humanity slip away. At first she didn't recognize what she felt as naked fury. At least she had been right about not having had sex with what bit her. She had been with the man she loved while it happened, and because of that he had been killed. A creature that raped and infected her stole his face. A little more of her humanity slipped away.

Nada leaned forward with one hand on the ground. She suddenly became aware of Grady asking her if she was OK, but she ignored him. She only had eyes for Kyros as she looked up sharply and glared at the manther. She slowly got to her feet and dug her fingernails into her palms as she fisted her hands. She looked at Kyros with a growing hatred she never knew possible. This creature had killed her beloved Derek and then stole his face. He had then turned her into whatever creature he was.

Nada could finally remember the pain. She never could grieve for Derek. The trauma of that night robbed her of all her memories of him and everyone else. When Kyros' blood finally reached her heart, she thought she dying. She rolled around in agony by that fire. When she finally awoke, all traces of Derek had been removed from the camp and her mind. She left Europe the next day, not remembering how she got there.

Kyros began to nod. "I see you finally remember."

"Why do you look like him?" She asked through clenched teeth. Nada moved a little closer and then edged to the side. She wanted him to move away from Grady.

"I can look like anybody, my love. So can you, but obviously you haven't realized your full potential yet. Don't worry, you will."

"Why do you look like him?" She slowly repeated.

"I like how it feels, and he was important to you."

"Why me?" She asked, fighting tears of rage.

"When I first spotted you in Greece, I knew my long search had finally ended. I followed you and your lover to Germany. I'll never forget how glorious you looked riding your stallion. I can still see the firelight reflecting off your damp skin." He paused to look at her a moment. "I've waited a long time for you."

"We never even spoke. How could you possibly know anything about me?" She asked and shook her head. She wished for her amnesia to end for so long, and now she wished for it to come back. She didn't know if she could handle all the memories that kept assaulting her. She began to remember all those full moons. She attracted all those animals and killed those that wouldn't leave her alone.

She looked at Grady, who came to that conclusion on his own. She glared at him, when she realized he ignored her yell to leave. She still dealt with losing Derek, so she didn't think she could handle losing Grady, too. She sucked in her breath and cringed as she remembered how she acted during the recent full moon. Her eyes filled with tears as she realized Grady had been right about her helping Kyros. She actually warned him that Grady approached. She groaned and looked back at Kyros. He stepped closer and held out a hand to caress her cheek. She hadn't even realized she let him get so close, but she stood her ground. Her breathing became irregular as she tried to remain calm. She looked him in the eyes, finally seeing a major difference between he and Derek. Kyros' eyes weren't human. They were gold with black slits.

"Everything had to match. You had to be the right age, and you had to have your 30th birthday on Friday the thirteenth during the full moon. Only then could the thirteen-day estrus follow. Everything had to align." *I can make my eyes look just like his, if you wish. I just prefer mine, as I prefer mating with you in my way. Before meeting you, I never had sex as a human, though I have to admit it was pleasurable.*

She gasped as she realized he said that last part in her head. It was just like in her dreams, though she could have done without the reminder of the night he killed Derek and then used her body. She tried to focus on what he said aloud. Everything had to align? Grady had been joking when he said that. Nada closed her eyes, trying to block out the voice.

*Why do you think of him? The two of you could never be together, my love. If you succeeded in mating with him, his child would die the instant you changed forms. Only my child would survive that.*

She reached up and covered her ears. "Get out of my head!" She screamed and then swung her arm out. It hit Kyros hard enough to push him back. "How could you know all that about me? That was three years ago."

He looked at her as if she were a child. "I just knew." The look irritated her, and she struck him again.

Grady stepped forward, expecting Kyros to attack her. Every instinct told him that he should leave, but he felt frozen to the spot. Nada looked like she was losing it and might need him. Her amnesia had been caused by the trauma of whatever Kyros did to her and someone named Derek. She obviously loved the man and he could tell it bothered her that Kyros looked like him. Now that her memory was back, would she still love Grady? He took another step closer. Kyros turned on him, when he sensed him approaching.

"No, you leave him alone!" Nada screamed and pictured the most aggressive animal she could think of. She didn't want to turn into the panther, so her body chose the next aggressive form. She felt her clothing rip as her body reshaped itself. Kyros looked at the wolf in shock.

"You've fed on lesser animals? How could you corrupt your blood line?" He stared at her with a mixture of shock and disgust. *I'm so disappointed in you.*

Nada attacked him and sunk her fangs into his neck. His scream turned into a roar as he *changed* into the panther and pushed her away. She knew he was stronger, but that couldn't stop her. She had to keep him away from Grady, as she jumped in front of him and growled at Kyros. Since she could no longer speak, she threw her thoughts at him, as he did earlier.

*Stay away from him, Kyros! I can't allow you to kill another man that I love.*

She realized her mistake at that admission as fire flew through his eyes. He roared and jumped at her. He slashed down her ribcage and threw her aside. She landed over twenty feet away and howled in pain. His claws were as sharp as razors, and blood flowed from her wounds.

Nada knew she would have to *change* in order to heal quickly, and that was all the time Kyros needed. Grady realized his time ran out. He tried to run, but Kyros jumped onto his back.

Grady screamed as his stitches ripped open. He rolled away in agony, and Kyros jumped on his chest, raking his claws down the front. The panther's jaws began to close around Grady's throat, about to break his neck.

Nada changed back to human and looked over to see Kyros gash Grady's chest and move closer to his throat. She felt the rage boiling over and soon all she saw was red. She felt her heart racing and the blood rushing through her veins. She was too far away to get there before Kyros could do his worst, so her body took over. She opened her mouth to scream and welcomed the feel of her fangs extending.

The scream was bloodcurdling and got both Grady's and Kyros' attention. Kyros jerked his head around to stare at Nada, who was beyond noticing her surroundings.

Without even realizing it was happening, Nada flew across the dock and landed on top of Kyros. She grabbed him around the chest and took off again. She flew them to the ship and dropped him on the deck. She landed a few feet away and held out her hands. She paid little attention to the talons at the end of her fingers. "I think I'm beginning to realize that potential you mentioned." She taunted him as new strength raced through her body, barely noticing her voice resonated deeply. Nada didn't have to look over her shoulder to know that wings grew out of her back. She could feel the muscles in her back flex each time the wings moved. She took aspects of the hawk, but the rest of her body remained human.  That her arms hadn't turned into the wings surprised her until she thought about the winged creature from her dream. It had flown at her but had also picked her up with its arms.  Maybe it was more related to her than she first thought. Nada ran her tongue over the two fangs in her upper jaw and smiled as she flexed her fingers. "Can you do this, Kyros?"

He growled low in his throat as he stared at her. She couldn't believe that was actually fear in his eyes. He slowly shook his head.

Nada was puzzled. If she could do it, why couldn't he?  "Do you still think I'm corrupted?" She threw his words back at him.

*I...I was told that you would be stronger than I am, but I refused to believe it. I can see now that I was wrong. I suppose there was much I wasn't told.*

"Who was it that told you about me?" She yelled at him.

*Why ask questions when you already know the answers?* He responded.

Nada took a deep breath and closed her eyes. When she opened them, she knelt in front of a campfire. She looked around and realized she was back in Germany, where Kyros first attacked her and Derek. Glancing around, she was relieved to see that Derek's remains were nowhere to be seen.

Nada groaned low in her throat and looked into the fire. What manner of dream was this? She wasn't even asleep.

*That's not necessary anymore.*

"Where are you!?" She screamed. "God, where are you?" She muttered. Nada licked and then bit her lower lip as she scanned her surroundings. She was still in her half-hawk/half-human shape and could feel her wings cut the air behind her. She crossed her arms over her chest and hugged herself. She never before felt so alone. "Why are you doing this to me?"

*Because you are my destiny.*

"Bullshit!" She seethed. "You don't even know what I am. I doubt you even know what created you." Nada tried to see through the darkness around her. "Did your creator find the dumbest animal he could to do his bidding?"

She expected some kind of reply but only silence greeted her. Since she wasn't asleep, Nada didn't know how to end whatever she experienced. "Did I strike a nerve there, *Kyros?* Where are you, coward?"

*I am sorry about your friend. Then again, maybe not.*

Nada lifted her gaze and glared across the darkness. She willed herself into dreams, so she damn well could will herself out of a daydream. She closed her eyes and screamed, "Grady!"

The world seemed to tilt for a second before Nada realized she was back on the dock. She focused on Grady lying in a growing pool of blood. She shook her head and wondered how long Kyros had managed to distract her.

"What are you waiting for?" She yelled at him. "You can only kill defenseless humans? No more, damn you!"

*I did not come here to kill you, my love, but what do you think those* defenseless *humans will do to you? Look at him.*

Kyros gestured to Grady, and Nada followed his gaze. Grady stared at her in shock.

*Look at his expression. He is terrified of you. He would probably be the first to agree that a creature like you should be killed. You are only safe with your own kind.*

Grady couldn't believe what he saw. At first he thought Kyros must have killed him and an angel had come for him. When he realized the angel was actually Nada, he focused on her. The dark brown wings had a span wider than he was tall. They rose at least two feet above her head, and they nearly touched the backs of her knees. As she stood across from the panther, the wings cut through the air behind her. With each angry stroke, feathers emerged under her arms and spread across her chest and then into her hair. A few moments later all of her hair shifted to feathers, and her fingers and toes were sharp like a bird's talons. Even in his weakened condition, he knew he would never see anything more beautiful.   Her pale naked skin made quite a contrast against the dark feathers and majestic wings.

Grady finally realized she had a one sided conversation with the panther.   Assuming Kyros answered her telepathically, he cringed when she glared in his direction. Even from that distance, he could tell there was something wrong with her eyes. They glowed with fury, and his jaw dropped.

The smile left Nada's face, and the wings beat faster.  She turned to Kyros and exposed her razor sharp teeth. He looked into her glowing eyes for a moment before looking at Grady again.

*That's right, my love, your place is with me. All he is good for is what is rushing through his veins, but it's OK to love your food.* Kyros mocked her. *Just don't play with it. Haven't you ever wondered what fresh blood from a human tasted like?*

Nada *had* wondered that very thing but shook her head. His soothing voice began to confuse her.  She couldn't be sure if it was his or her own inner voice talking.

*Stop fighting your nature, my love. If you can't kill it, I'll be happy to do it for you. I owe him a death.*

Kyros turned toward Grady with a roar and pounced. She felt frozen to the spot and couldn't move at first. Then she caught Grady's gaze. The pool of blood was much larger now, and she couldn't bear to see it get any bigger. She then saw Grady shut his eyes in defeat, and her temper flared. Nada shook her head and yelled.

"No!"

She flew after Kyros and grabbed him before either of them could blink. They were less than ten feet from Grady, who closed his eyes in preparation of his own death. Nada tore open Kyros' throat with her fangs and fed on him.

When the attack didn't occur, Grady slowly opened his eyes. He couldn't see very well, but what he could see were her wings. They curled around both Nada and the panther, so he couldn't see what she did. What he heard was worse than anything, and he wished for the strength to cover his ears.

As the blood coursed through Nada's body, the animal instinct within her subsided. As rational thought returned, she realized what she did. She had already been polluted with enough of Kyros' blood, so she pushed him away. She then scratched his neck and chest with her talons before shoving him away. Nada crouched down and watched as the rest of his blood drained onto the dock. She needed to make sure he didn't *morph* to save himself.

"You don't know anything about humans, Kyros. Just because you feed on us, and kill us, and try to live as one of us, it doesn't mean you know a damn thing. You'd have to have a soul, which you will soon die without."

*Not everyone has a soul, my love, but yours is very old.*

Nada rolled her eyes. "When you saw me in Greece, you should have kept on walking." The hatred and anger and hurt finally came to the surface and erupted in heaving sobs. She wanted to kick him until all her pain went away, but she knew that would never happen. She took deep breaths and tried to calm down.

*I could no sooner pass you by than stop breathing or eating. The creator told me that it would come to this. He knew you were the one. I cannot look like him, but I guess he knew you could. He told me that you were my destiny.*

She thought about that for a moment before shaking her head. "Then I guess it was fated for me to kill you." She responded bitterly, wishing she hadn't heard what he just said. Could the "creator" see into the future? Was he the one giving her the dreams? He obviously was the one who knew about her 30th birthday aligning. She tried to shut out Kyros' voice as he continued but couldn't.

*If our mating doesn't produce offspring, you only have one more chance. I know you want a child, my love. The dreams were sent to you for a reason. Go back to Greece. Once you're home, you'll know where to go.*

He got her interest with that. "Is that where this creator is? What is it?" She remembered the cave and wondered if that had been in Greece. If that was where Kyros considered home, it must be.

Kyros reached for her as his paw changed into a human hand. She fought the impulse to move out of his reach but cringed as his hand moved behind her neck. He pulled her closer, and she was forced to look into his golden eyes. She heard his voice inside her head one last time.

*Since it helped me create you, just look inside yourself. You've seen him before, but this will help.*

As she looked into his eyes, she saw flashes of something indescribable but somehow familiar. The images were dark and vague, but they scared her. It was too much like her dream, but this time she almost saw the face. She blinked several times before finally pushing away from him with a yell. She shook her head, trying to dislodge what she just saw from her mind. The glowing eyes had been the worst part.

Kyros closed his eyes, and she heard no more. She jumped back as if burnt, as the memory of their mating clicked into place. After she flew to the park, she landed in a tree. Her body knew that Kyros was close by and took over. She changed into the panther, and Kyros found her a moment later. He mated with her just like he had in her first dream of him.

"Nada?"

She looked toward the voice and stared at Grady. The pool of blood around him began to darken. Since she still had the wings, she flew back to him.

"Grady." She yelled, still crying. She sat beside him and pulled him into her arms. "Don't die, Grady."

She was barely aware of the wings merging back into her body, but Grady watched as the feathers on her head returned to her normal hair. He looked into her eyes. They weren't glowing anymore, but the gold with black slits chilled him. He reached up and touched her smooth cheek, which was covered with blood. He knew she had no idea how she looked, but he still thought her beautiful.

"I love you, Nada. I'm sorry I didn't listen to you." He paused to take in a shaky breath. "Who's going to look after you now?"

Nada wiped away the blood that trickled out of the side of his mouth. For the first time she wasn't tempted by blood. She hoped it was because she was too worried about him, and not that she just fed on Kyros. She shook her head as the tears flowed down her cheeks. "Don't talk like that. I'm amazed you can still look at me, let alone want to look after me. How can you love me after all that you witnessed tonight?"

Grady shook his head and grimaced. "I've practically loved you since you were brought in as that damn wounded cat. You haven't done anything since then to make me not love you." He groaned and more blood trickled down his cheek. "You've made me a better person, and I was looking forward to what you would show me next." He winced as a stab of pain went through him.

"I can save you, Grady." She hated to say it, but she hated the thought of losing him more. Since she finally remembered how Kyros infected her, she knew that her blood could save Grady.

"I'd have to be like you, though?" He asked as his eyes went in and out of focus. It got harder to keep them open. He had the vague realization that he was dying.

"Yes," she cried. "I'll only do it you want me to. I love you, too." She caressed his face and kissed his forehead. She wanted to convince him to stay with her. If they were both alike, she could have his children. They might actually have a life together. She may have made him a better person, but that paled next to what he had done for her. He taught her how to love again, not only him but also herself. He helped her take back her life. Instead of watching television, her spare time had been spent with him. She couldn't imagine going back to that old life again. She didn't even miss the escape her dreams used to give her. Many thoughts went through her head, but she held her tongue. She couldn't be selfish. It had to be his decision.

He shook his head and swallowed the lump in his throat. "I know how hard it is for you, and you're stronger than I am. I don't think I could handle it."

"How can you say that? I'm not strong." Her emotions got the better of her, and she decided to plead with him. "Please stay with me, Grady. Don't leave me alone again." She begged, but he closed his eyes.

"You're stronger than you think." His voice was so soft that she barely heard him.

"Grady?" She shook him, but he didn't stir. "Grady?" She yelled louder but still nothing. Nada threw back her head and screamed, "Grady!" She let her grief consume her, and the tears flowed freely.

"What the hell?" A new voice exclaimed.

Nada looked toward the voice. Tears blurred her vision, so she ran a hand across her eyes. She cleared the tears but wasn't aware she smeared Grady's and Kyros' blood across her face. She finally recognized Detective Somerset. He had his gun drawn and pointed at her. She looked behind him to see several cars pulling up.

"What happened here?" Cayle asked as he looked around. He looked from the dead dockworker, to Grady and finally to Nada.

"There's a dead panther behind us. It killed that man over there and then attacked Grady. I killed it when it tried to escape." She explained to him.

The detective walked closer and crouched down in front of Nada and Grady. He felt for a pulse on Grady and then pulled a cell phone from his jacket. He then took off the jacket and placed it around Nada's shoulders. It reminded her of being naked, but she couldn't take her arms away from Grady to put them into the sleeves of the jacket.

After calling for an ambulance, Cayle turned back to Nada. She looked at the people approaching and didn't pay Cayle any attention. He looked from the blood and her tears into her eyes and gasped. She looked back to him and saw the shock in his gaze as he stared at her eyes. As she wondered what was wrong, she ran her tongue over her teeth. When she realized her fangs hadn't changed back to normal teeth yet, she remembered the creature's glowing eyes. Was that what Cayle saw in her? She groaned softly.

"What are you?" Cayle asked.

Nada closed her eyes as she concentrated. When she looked back at him, everything was back to normal. "Just someone trying to survive. Can you help him, Cayle?" Fresh tears began to flow as she clung tighter to Grady.

Cayle could only blink, and neither of them paid attention as the dock became congested with people.

# Chapter Twenty-Two

The next few weeks passed in a blur for Nada. She tried to return to the life that she led when she had amnesia but found that very difficult. She was no longer that girl. She continued working at the hospital, determined to get closer to the people she worked with. Mia had always been a friend, but they hardly ever did anything together away from the hospital. Nada intended to change that. She held up her end of the bargain and doubled with Zack, Mia and Jamal. Surprisingly enough, she had fun.

The ambulance took Grady to the hospital where she worked. He surprised everyone and survived his attack, though he needed many blood transfusions. She visited as often as she could. Her first visit had been painful for her, since he was as pale as she. Nada slowly approached his bedside and took one of his limp hands within hers. Her hand was much smaller, though his looked frailer.

"Oh, Grady," she sobbed. "I need your advice. Hell, I need *you!*" How she wished he would open his eyes and look at her. She should have told him about the winged creature when she had the chance. She didn't know how she could have convinced herself that it wasn't relevant. Could it have been that she feared admitting it aloud that the creature might be a part of her? She couldn't have known that, since she hadn't even met Kyros yet. True, she dreamt of him, but that wasn't the same thing. Who or what gave her those dreams?

Would she really have to go to Greece to get the answers? She didn't want to go. She learned too much about herself already.

She looked at Grady and ran a hand down his cheek. "I'm sorry I wasn't able to protect you from him. I'm sorry for so many things." She wiped a stray tear away. She was mostly sorry for telling him no while they were at the hotel. Maybe if she got pregnant with his child, her heat would have ended, and Kyros would have gone away. She doubted it would have been that simple though, since nothing ever was.

She continued to visit him at the beginning and end of every shift. She would talk to him for hours, not minding he wasn't conscious for any of it. The doctors were pessimistic that he would ever come out of the coma, but she knew he was strong. That he survived at all was proof enough for her.

Nada spent a lot of time over the next two weeks sitting across from Detective Cayle Somerset's desk. He had her recount that night over and over again. She figured he wanted to see if she would slip up, but it might have been to just convince himself that it actually happened. His rational mind couldn't let him believe that the beautiful fragile woman sitting across from him was anything other than what she appeared.

During one of those discussions, Cayle dropped the bomb that the panther's blood exactly matched the blood taken from Grady's clinic floor. She just shrugged and asked how that mattered.

"How does it matter?" He asked incredulously. "That panther was locked in that busted cage, wasn't it?"

Nada shrugged again. "How would I know what was in the cage? You'd have to ask Grady."

"Yes, but I can't do that right now, can I?" He replied.

Nada looked at her hands and frowned. "That's not my fault. I tried to protect him." Even as she said it, she felt guilty. She got him involved in the first place. She looked up and shot Cayle an accusing look. "You're the one who called and told him about the ship."

"It's good that you brought that up. Why *did* you want to know about ships leaving to Europe? How did you know that the damn panther would be there?"

As she looked into his eyes, she thought about Grady. "I had a dream," she said quietly, and her eyes misted. "All you had to do was wait for me to call you back, but instead you called Grady. He feared the worst and drove out there. I was going to take care of the panther on my own, since I knew..." She stopped. Nada bit her lip at her near slip. She couldn't reveal too much.

"You knew what?" He asked with a gentler tone. He still dealt with his own guilt over calling Grady.

She moved her hands to her mouth and closed her eyes. She again wondered what those dreams meant. Was it Kyros' creator speaking to her, or her own subconscious trying to give her hints about what happened to her? The last dream stood out the most, since it told of the future. The creature from the cave must have given her that one, but why? As she thought about it, she realized that she wouldn't have gone to the shipyard if not for that dream. She also wouldn't have called Cayle for help. The dream made that future a reality to her, so it made her more of a puppet to some higher purpose. It sickened her that she had played right into its hands.

The rest of the dreams didn't make any sense. A few of them had seemed so real, that it took her awhile to realize she dreamed them. Those all took place in Germany by those mountains and the lake, which were from her past. Then she thought about the dream with the creature in it. That had been the only one that wasn't by the mountains. She had never been in a cave, and she never met any winged creature. She didn't know where that one came from, and she wasn't sure if she was supposed to have seen it. She willed herself into having the dream, so she could fantasize about Grady. Nada suddenly realized the difference. She didn't prompt the dreams she had of the past and future, so she was shown things about herself and Kyros. The other ones were dreams she went into on her own, so in a way she controlled them. Could she see things that she wasn't supposed to see? That gave her new insight into her abilities. Would she be able to get some of her answers by making herself dream about them, or would that only have worked if Kyros still lived? No, she told herself, she had the feeling that his creator had more to do with it. Of course, she could no longer remember what it looked like, except for those god-awful wings. She thought about it for a moment. Would she really want to see it again? She put away the sketchpad so she wouldn't have to look at the drawing she did, though she couldn't tear it up. Kyros referred to his creator as a male. Could he have used Kyros just to get to her? Maybe he was unable to take the form of a man to be able to blend into society as Kyros did. Even a panther was more acceptable than a creature so hideous that her own subconscious wouldn't allow her to keep its memory. Nada shook her head in frustration.

She looked at Cayle. It felt as if she had been silent forever, but she knew only a minute went by. He waited for an answer, but she didn't quite know how to word it.

Her thoughts went back to her dream of the shipyard and the future. She knew Kyros would be there and that Grady would be pulled away from her. Kyros most likely gave her the dreams where they were together by the lake. If she wasn't willing to find her answers in her dreams, where did she have to turn? Kyros' words echoed inside her head.

*We're not the last...Go back to Greece. Once you're home, you'll know where to go.*

Did she want the answers badly enough to go back there? Dreaming would be safer. They wouldn't be pleasant, but definitely safer.

"You knew what?" Cayle asked again.

Nada looked back into his eyes. He had been in that last dream as well as Zack. They both approached her with open arms. Half the dream already happened because of her, so should she believe in what she felt? She instinctively knew she could trust Cayle, and she had always liked Zack. She would have to see what came of getting to know them both better.

"I knew he would get hurt." She finally answered.

"Because of your dream? Was I in this dream?" Her eyes widened, and he smiled. "I wondered why it was me that you called. We didn't exactly hit it off at your boyfriend's clinic."

She almost told him that Grady wasn't her boyfriend but held her tongue. She actually liked the sound of it, but then thought of Derek. A stab of guilt flashed through her as she remembered the phone call she made a week earlier. Nada only met his parents once, so they had no idea how to get hold of her. As far as they knew, both she and Derek disappeared during their trip to Europe. Even though it hadn't been Nada's fault that she lost her memory, it was nearly unbearable to hear his mother sob as she told her what happened to Derek. Not being able to bury her son left her without closure. Nada hoped to never have to feel the pain of losing a child and shook herself of the memory. She looked up and met Cayle's steady gaze.

"You're the only cop I know." She told him, but his look told her he wasn't buying it. "Well, who else could I have called who could find out ship schedules?"

"The dream wasn't that specific, huh?" He asked.

"Are they ever?" She countered.

Cayle finally smiled showing a wide expanse of white teeth. "I just wonder if I had your blood tested, would it be like that panther's?"

The question startled her, and she gasped. "No, of course not. He was a panther, and I'm human."

He nodded. "You know that's not what I meant. I didn't imagine how your eyes looked that night, did I? The panther had the same eyes. You tell me how a human can have the same eyes as a panther."

"Maybe you didn't see what you think you saw." Her lower lip quivered with fear. Nada thought about what he said. Grady must have seen her eyes like that as well, but he hadn't commented. Since he hadn't been afraid of her, maybe he couldn't focus on them. At least she could be thankful for that. Nada looked back at Cayle. "Was my dream wrong about you?"

He closed the file in front of him and sat back in his chair. The look he gave her made her nervous. She was glad when he dropped his gaze back to his desk and shook his head. Cayle handed the file to her. "What do you think?"

Nada opened the file and read the report. Cayle watched her silently. Being such a big man, he had always been protective of small women. For some unknown reason he felt particularly protective of Nada. He wondered if Dr. Duncan felt the same way. Being around Nada probably wasn't good for his health, but he felt confident he could take care of himself. He wished the doctor would wake up, since he had a list of questions for him. Cayle continued to watch the woman pouring over his report.

Nada was oblivious of the man across from her as she read. Nothing mentioned her eyes or teeth being different or the fact she had been nude. According to the report, Dr. Duncan received a phone call that a panther was spotted on the docks. He and his girlfriend drove out there in time to see the panther kill a dockworker. The panther then turned on Grady, and she killed it. Nada looked back at Cayle, thankful he didn't show up when she had the wings. She doubted he'd be able to overlook those. She was still coming to grips with her newest ability, along with trying to avoid thinking of where it came from. "Thank you."

"Don't thank me, yet."

The ominous way he spoke sent chills down her spine. "What do you mean?"

Cayle stared at her for a moment and then pulled open a drawer. He pulled out another file and placed it in front of him on the desk. Nada didn't look at it but kept her gaze locked on him.

He tapped the file. "I searched Dr. Duncan's clinic. I had to cover all bases and had to make sure there wasn't anything there about the panther. I didn't find anything on that, but this got my attention." He held up the file, since she still hadn't looked at it.

Nada tore her gaze away from him and looked at the file. She saw it enough to recognize it as her medical record. Grady kept a log of everything that happened.

She never read any of it, so she could only hope he'd been cryptic. Cayle's next comment confirmed her hope.

"He wrote most of it in some kind of code, but the N.B. got my attention. So did the blood sample. Of course, the lab is convinced it was contaminated, but what got my attention was that the same unknown blood that was in the panther is also in this sample. Is this your file, Nada?" Cayle asked.

Nada blinked a few times before looking at him. She didn't know if she could lie, so she just shook her head. "Grady ran a veterinarian clinic, Detective. Why would my medical record be there?" She hedged.

"So the N.B. doesn't stand for Nada Berch? And didn't I tell you to call me Cayle?" He reminded her.

She shook her head. "Kind of hard to call you that when I'm being interrogated, *Detective*."

He looked down at his desk and tapped a pencil against the file. A smile slowly crept across his face. He really wished he didn't like her. "That's the report that I'm filing, Nada. I was just hoping you could clear up a few things for me, that's all."

He held out his hand and she gave him the file. He placed it on top of her medical record. "I don't want to mess things up for you, but you'll be seeing a lot of me from now on." He said, trying to make it sound threatening.

Nada sighed and then beamed at him. "Well, I had planned on that."

When she got home, Nada went to the bathroom to splash water on her face. Her body always ran a little hot, but the extra stress made it harder to handle. As she stared at her reflection, she focused on the water droplets sliding down her face. In the last week she tried not to think about what happened to her three years ago. The memory of Derek had been too painful, which was why she waited to call his parents. He had been her first love. She shook her head as she pictured his face, something she had been unable to do since his tragic death. Kyros hadn't looked exactly like him, of course. The evil inside him distorted Derek's face, especially when he used his own golden eyes. Derek had been caring and loving, and that was how she wanted to remember him.

Nada focused on the mirror in front of her and got a major shock. She didn't recognize her own reflection.

"What the hell?" She jumped back and hit the wall behind her. The strange reflection mimicked her movements. Nada slowly approached the mirror and touched the glass, half expecting her hand to keep going and touch flesh. She moved her hand away from the mirror and reached up to touch her new mouth. She hadn't even been aware of *morphing*, but that was what she did. As she looked closer, her eyes filled with tears. She looked from her black hair to her blue eyes. She couldn't turn into a man as she told Grady, but she looked like Derek. Then she realized she still looked like herself as well. Was this what their daughter would have looked like? The child she would never have? A single tear escaped and rolled down her left cheek. She would have been beautiful.

Nada then thought of Grady. She wished she could have had his child, but she would never know what that child would look like. As she pictured Grady's face, she began to *morph* again. Only this time, she was able to watch it. She smiled, as her hair became curly and lightened in color. She looked into her eyes, which changed from blue to a hazel-green. "Oh, my God," she breathed. How was she able to *change* into Grady, since she never fed from him? Then she realized that Kyros fed from him as he tried to kill him. She then fed from Kyros as he died. Nada picked up some of the curly hair and pulled on it, which was still as long as her own hair. At least she would always have Grady with her. She shook her head in disbelief. She finally noticed she was taller and laughed.

Another week passed before Nada could stop denying the possibility she was pregnant. She bought a home test to confirm it. She still held the positive response in her hand, when someone rang her doorbell. Too shocked to put it down before answering, Cayle walked in and spotted the test in her hand.

"Are congratulations in order?" He asked.

She shrugged. "I suppose." Nada looked back at the pink plus sign.

"Well, I'm sorry you and Dr. Duncan can't celebrate together." He responded.

Nada sat on the couch, too surprised to think before she spoke. "He's not the father."

Cayle could only stare at her. She didn't know what to do. She wanted children, but could she have Kyros' child? She remembered everything he told her, including how she wouldn't be able to carry a normal child to term. Could she abort, knowing she may never have another child? Kyros told her she only had one more chance. He mentioned coming back in three years if he wasn't able to mate with her. Was that the last chance she had? When she was 33, would she have another thirteen-day heat? Would someone else come to mate with her, possibly Kyros' creator? She doubted that, since he didn't come in the first place. It was more likely that he would find another disciple to do his bidding. There were so many questions and no answers.  Nada dropped her head into her hands and rubbed her temples.

"Did Grady know?" Cayle finally asked.

"I don't know...I don't think so." Nada responded without looking up.  Grady knew that if she got close to Kyros during her heat, that she *changed*.  Since that didn't happen when she arrived at the dock, Grady would have concluded the same that she had. "He might have." She muttered as tears filled her eyes. Would she ever get the chance to ask him?

Nada wiped her eyes and looked up at Cayle. "What are you doing here?" She finally thought to ask.

He shrugged and sat across from her.  "I just wanted to let you know that the report has been filed. The lab is still working on the panther, but you're pretty much out of it now."

For the first time since meeting him, Nada really looked at Cayle. She smiled as she realized she never noticed his appearance.  He was dark-skinned and built like a football player, so she figured he must work out at the gym.  His black hair was cut close to his scalp, and his eyes were so dark she could barely make out his pupils. He wasn't quite as tall as Grady but was at least six feet. Nada had to admit he was an attractive man. She couldn't even guess his age, but figured he had to be in his thirties. "You could have called and told me that, Detective."

He fidgeted a little and smiled. "I know.  I guess I was worried about you and wanted to make sure you were alright."

Nada thought about her pregnancy again. She was only three weeks, but she could tell it was farther along than that. Animals weren't pregnant for as long as humans.  How would she explain giving birth in less than nine months?  She looked back at Cayle, who leaned forward in his seat watching her.

"Cayle, if I needed your help with something very sensitive, could I count on you?" She asked.

He raised his eyebrows.  "How sensitive?"

She bit the inside of her lower lip and shrugged.  "I think I'm going to need help when I give birth.  I'm going to need somebody who'll be willing to write out a birth certificate without any questions or a thorough examination of the baby."

"You mean no blood drawn?"  He pressed.

She nodded.  "From both of us."

Cayle took a deep breath and let it out slowly.  "What am I getting myself into here, Nada?"

"I don't want you to do anything that you don't want to do, Cayle.  I just need your help with this.  If you're not willing, I'll manage somehow."

"You're not a sheep in wolf's clothing are you?"  He asked after a moment.

"What do you mean?"  Nada asked, but it was her turn to fidget.

He looked her over for a moment and then pointed to her.  "Look in the mirror.  You're so tiny and fragile looking.  I can't imagine you being able to hurt anything, but I've seen that damn panther, Nada. According to the lab report, it was torn apart by an unidentified animal.  You've told me that you killed it.  Now, if that isn't a contradiction, what is?  You don't want your blood drawn, and you don't want your child's blood drawn.  If I help you, could people get hurt?"

She quickly shook her head.  "This is to protect me and my unborn child.  I've never nor will I ever hurt another human being.  You have to believe that, Cayle. Trust your instincts."  Tears misted the corners of her eyes. "I'm trusting mine by asking for your help. I'm not asking you to break the law, just bend it a little."

He smiled at her last remark. "I have a friend that's a doctor. He'll have to verify that you gave birth, but I'll have him waive any blood typing."

She sighed. "Thank you."

On her way home from work that night, Nada stopped off at the ATM to get some money. Surprised to see another woman at the machine, she glanced at the clock in the dashboard. Realizing it wasn't as late as it usually would be when she got off work, she remembered she left early. Morning sickness certainly didn't happen only in the morning.

She just pulled up, when she saw the woman being attacked by a mugger. Nada got out of the car and bit her lip. She didn't know if she should get involved, since she had more than her own life to consider now. The man striking the woman made up Nada's mind. She ran over and jumped on his back. He spun on her and hit her in the temple with his gun. As she fell beside the woman on the ground, he took off. Nada reached over to the woman and helped her up.

"Are you alright?"

"Yes, but he took everything." She cried hysterically, cupping her face with her palm. The woman had a gash just below her eyebrow. Nada seethed with anger.

"Don't worry." She looked to where the man fled. "I'll get him." Nada ran behind the nearest building and stripped. She shouldn't be doing what she was about to do, but something needed to be done. As she pictured Kyros and his creator in her mind, she began to *change*.

She wasn't even sure if she could do it again but actually smiled when she felt the wings.

She fought for control, so that she would only partially *change*. She could do without the talons and fangs this time. She flew through the air as feathers protruded to cover her in all the right areas. This time, Nada looked over her shoulder and stared in awe at the huge wings. They weren't as large as the beast from her dream, but they were close. Nada saw the man running through the park in the distance. She flew at him and was on him in an instant and shoved him to the ground. Making sure she kept his face buried in the dirt, she sat on his back.

"You've been a bad boy," Nada spoke but didn't even recognize her voice. She pulled the purse from his grasp and then smacked him on the back of the head. She checked her surroundings to make sure no one was around. A man and woman approached from a distance, but they wouldn't be able to see her clearly. Knowing that the mugger would be unconscious for a while, she flew off.

Nada landed behind the building where she left her clothing. She pictured her human body and closed her eyes as the wings merged with her back. She donned her clothes quickly and walked back to where the woman still sat crying. The whole episode took less than ten minutes. Nada handed the woman her purse and then reached into her own purse for her cell phone. She called Cayle and told him about the man in the park.

"You better hurry, since I wouldn't want him waking up before you can arrest him. I'm sure the lady with me will be happy to press charges." She looked at the lady in question, who still stared at her returned purse. At least she stopped crying.

"What happened?" Cayle responded.

"Uh, I'll try to explain later." Of course, when later happened, the explanation was not to Cayle's satisfaction. The man he arrested was wanted in a few states for not only robbery but also rape. Nada helped apprehend a very dangerous man, who had no idea what happened to him. All he knew was that something attacked him from behind. When he woke up, he was in jail. The only eyewitnesses to the event were too far away to see much, but they said it looked like a "large bird" attacked him. Nada barely listened as Cayle told her that the witnesses were movie stars. When she realized he asked a question, she looked puzzled.

"What?"

"I asked if you were going to see their movie?"

When she still looked blank, he continued. "*An Enemy's Kiss*? Haven't you heard of it?"

She shook her head and made no comment. She was a little distracted to care who witnessed the attack. Nada was just thankful they had been so far away.

"Well, I'm going to treat this like the panther." Cayle told Nada after the man had been placed in that jail cell. "It's just another contradiction, isn't it? How could you catch up to him and tackle him? Let alone be confused with a large bird. You can't even weigh a hundred pounds."

"109 actually." She had gained a few pounds since she got pregnant.

"You're pregnant, for Christ's sake!" He countered, as if reading her mind.

She didn't respond but smiled instead. She liked how it felt to put that criminal down. Maybe she could do good things with her abilities after all. She needed to do something to make up for all the evil that Kyros did.

# Epilogue

## Six months later

Nada pushed the stroller through the park. She headed to the open field where they set up the football field. When she spotted the men, Nada waved. Zack and Cayle left their team and ran over.

"I'm not late am I?" Nada asked them when they were close enough to hear.  She looked over at the sidelines, where blankets and chairs were being placed.

"No, you're right on time," Zack responded as he knelt in front of the double stroller. Nada looked at her son and daughter, who were born just over two weeks earlier. They loved Zack, who was the doctor who delivered them. Surprise was an understatement, when Nada found out that he had been the friend Cayle mentioned.

"Good. I stopped by Kiefer's and thought for sure I would miss your kick off." Nada leaned down and put the pacifier back into Dawn's mouth. She then pulled the blanket up to Drew's chin, who slept on undisturbed.

"Did you go by and see Grady?"

"No, I'll go by after this.  I just wanted to make sure the new vet was handling things." She responded as she looked away from her children. Kiefer Taylor took his friendship with Grady seriously. Grady took care of his clinic while he was away, so Kiefer returned the favor.

Dr. Taylor hired a temporary veterinarian to work at Grady's clinic until he came out of the coma. The new vet seemed nice, although a bit young.

"Well, she's not exactly new anymore. She's past the 90 day probationary period." He added with a mischievous smile.

Nada shrugged and tried unsuccessfully to return the smile. "It's just not the same without Grady there."

"How is he?" Cayle asked.

Nada straightened and sighed. "There's been no change since the machines were shut off, but at least he's breathing on his own."

"That's a good sign though, right?" Cayle asked and looked at Zack.

Dr. Thorton shrugged. "Well, his body has repaired most of the damage that was done to it, but the initial blood loss cut off oxygen to his brain. That damage may never repair itself." He looked at Nada and gave her a hopeful smile. "He's doing better than any of us expected, so who knows?"

The men were called back to the game, and Nada pushed the stroller over to where Mia spread out a blanket. After making sure both babies were OK, Nada sat beside Mia. They got quite close over the last six months, and Nada could finally consider them good friends. Mia and Jamal broke up a few months earlier, and Mia expressed interest in Cayle.

Nada settled into a comfortable dating relationship with Zack before finding out that he and Cayle were friends. She convinced Zack to invite the detective to dinner with them, and Nada invited Mia. The two hit it off immediately, and they all double dated quite often since then.

Nada could no longer hide her pregnancy at three months. She had an ultrasound, which revealed twins at twenty weeks. Knowing then that she would give birth three months ahead of schedule, she told everyone she was five months pregnant. She also stopped her continued efforts with the criminals around town. Her protruding stomach affected her balance, and she also didn't want to take any more chances with their lives. She could wait until after they were born to resume her continued fight against crime. Nada always called Cayle when she apprehended someone, and he became known for his high arrest count. Since he became a close friend of hers, she trusted him more and more. She even felt that someday soon, she would reveal her entire situation to him.

Since having twins early was normal, no one questioned her giving birth at eight months, which was actually only six. Both babies were perfect in every way, but it worried Nada. Would they continue to grow faster than humans did? Would she have to worry how they would relate to each other as they matured? Nada knew animals didn't even acknowledge incest, and it seemed too perfect that she had a boy and a girl. Was there some higher purpose to everything that happened or was it just fate?

The thing that worried her the most was would they be just like their parents? Would they have a thirst for blood and be able to change into other animals? She knew that Kyros' blood along with her own were now in both their children, so they should have the same abilities she had. She currently breast-fed them, so they continued to get whatever she took in. What would happen when she weaned them? Their father had been a vicious killer, so would they take after him? She could only hope that being raised by a loving mother would curb their aggressive natures. If she could do it, so could they. She had hopes they would someday help her keep their city safe.

Nada tried to stop worrying about it, and looked at her children. They appeared so peaceful, that she couldn't imagine them being like Kyros. As she looked from Drew's dark head to Dawn's light one, Nada smiled as Mia made a comment about how gorgeous they were. Then she noted how big they were for their age, and Nada bit back the cringe. She just smiled and nodded. "Yes, everyone says that," was her rehearsed response.

Nada looked back at the game. Zack caught her gaze and waved. She smiled and waved back. She watched the two friends playing football. They were about as opposite as two men could get. Zack's hair was still long and Cayle's still closely cropped. One was a doctor and the other a cop. She couldn't even imagine what they had in common, but they were both exceptional men.

She turned to look at Mia, who had both hands cupped around her mouth, shouting encouragement for her man. When she noticed Nada staring at her, Mia turned to her with a wink. Nada smiled. "So, how are things going with you and Cayle?"

"Oh, girl, let me tell ya. He is *soooooo* sweet. I can't thank you enough for fixin' us up."

Nada leaned back and propped herself up on her arms. "No problem. You deserve to be with someone who treats you right." She had no doubt that Cayle would do just that. She looked back at the game, and her gaze went to Zack. She never thought they'd be anything other than work colleagues.

Nada and Zack were surprised when Cayle got them together, especially since they already knew each other. They had been dating for about two months, when the detective brought his doctor friend by her apartment. It wasn't exactly the way she wanted Zack to find out about her pregnancy, but she assured him that she had nothing to do with the father. Even after six months, their relationship remained platonic, which was fine with Nada. She had a feeling it wasn't fine with Zack, but he didn't press her. She had a lot of mental wounds that needed to heal before she could let herself become intimately involved with another man.

After the game, Nada left for the hospital to see Grady. The twins slept the whole time, which made it easier for her to visit. Grady slept on undisturbed, even though Nada talked to him as if he were awake.

"You should see them, Grady. They're so big." Nada paused and looked at his peaceful face. So many times, she just looked at him and thought he would open his eyes and look at her. She would even welcome his suspicious gaze, just so that he would look at her. She reached out and softly caressed his cheek. "Come back to me, Grady."

Nada gazed across the room and stared at her sleeping children. Sometimes she regretted that she and Grady never slept together. It would have been much nicer to have his children than Kyros'. She looked back at Grady. "If you can hear me, just know that I'll always love you. Whenever you choose to come back to me, I'll be here." She leaned forward and pressed her cheek to his chest. She closed her eyes and listened to his heartbeat.

As she remembered the last time her face had been against his chest, she groaned low in her throat. If only she hadn't pushed him away after their kiss. They would have made love, and she may have conceived. It was finally possible for her not to *change* if she was careful. Ever since Kyros' death, she was able to prevent *changing* during the full moon. As long as she always got enough blood and unless she wanted to, there would never be the need to *change*. She finally felt it was well worth the risk for the chance of having a normal baby, especially since discovering she could partially *change*, which shouldn't effect a fetus. Of course, she didn't know that for sure, as she didn't know that her twins wouldn't be normal. And as a tear slipped down her cheek to fall on Grady, she didn't even know if or when he would wake up.

Only time would tell, but then *that* is another part of the myth.

www.ingramcontent.com/pod-product-compliance
Lightning Source LLC
Chambersburg PA
CBHW020244150626
46552CB00020B/97